15/5/14

D1433382

C333303543

# A Fabulous Liar

# A Fabulous Liar

## SUSANN PÁSZTOR

*Translated by Shaun Whiteside*

Atlantic Books
London

First published in Germany in 2010 by Kiepenheuer & Witsch Verlag, GmbH & Co. KG.

First published in Great Britain in 2013 by Atlantic Books, an imprint of Atlantic Books Ltd.

Copyright © Susann Pásztor, 2010
Translator Copyright © Shaun Whiteside, 2013

The moral right of Susann Pásztor to be identified as the author of this work has been asserted by her in accordance with the Copyright, Designs and Patents Act of 1988.

The moral right of Shaun Whiteside to be identified as the translator of this work has been asserted by him in accordance with the Copyright, Designs and Patents Act of 1988.

All rights reserved. No part of this publication
may be reproduced, stored in a retrieval system or transmitted
in any form or by any means, electronic, mechanical, photocopying,
recording or otherwise, without the prior permission of both
the copyright owner and the above publisher of this book.

This novel is entirely a work of fiction. The names, characters and incidents portrayed
in it are the work of the author's imagination and not to be construed as real. Any resemblance to
actual persons, living or dead, events or localities, is entirely coincidental.

The translation of this work was supported by a grant from the Goethe-Institut
which is funded by the German Ministry of Foreign Affairs

1 3 5 7 9 10 8 6 4 2

A CIP catalogue record for this book is available from the British Library.

Hardback ISBN: 978 1 84887 848 8
EBook ISBN: 978 1 78239 143 2

Set in 12.5/15pt Granjon
Designed by Nicky Barneby @ Barneby Ltd
Printed by the MPG Printgroup

Atlantic Books
An imprint of Atlantic Books Ltd
Ormond House
26–27 Boswell Street
London WC1N 3JZ

www.atlantic-books.co.uk

# *Prologue*

ONE SUNNY AUTUMN MORNING in September 1959, József Molnár prepared to put an end to his life. The previous evening, in a station bar, he had sought suitable words of farewell for his loved ones, and posted the three letters. He booked himself into a city-centre hotel that he knew from previous visits. It let rooms by the hour, and was in a former underground air-raid shelter. After he had choked down several sleeping tablets with a little water, he lay down on the once-pink bedcover, studied the mould stains and the flaking plaster on the ceiling, listened to the dripping tap and the traffic trundling away above his head, and waited for death.

But what he took for dying was only another beginning of the end, and instead of death the landlord appeared, followed by a gruff emergency doctor, because József had only been able to pay for two hours, and that wasn't long enough to die. And so it was that the following day three people gathered around a different bed – a hospital bed this time, with clean white sheets – gazing with concern at József's pale, exhausted face. (He had every reason to look pale and exhausted. Stomach pumping is no small matter, and neither is a failed suicide, especially since its cause had not yet been erased from the world.)

It was three women who were bending over him, all careful to keep their distance from one another. Two of them had never met before and never would again. Both were pregnant. One was about to give birth, while the other had known only for a few days that she was expecting, and was full of expectations in fact because there was nothing that she wanted more than this tired, skinny man who would rather have been dead. The third already had a child by him. The child was twelve years old and far from happy.

They were all crying, because each of them had reason enough. After all, one had nearly lost her husband, the other the one she finally wanted to marry, and the third an ex-husband from whom she had once separated with the heaviest of hearts and despite a powerful sense of commitment. They sobbed with pain and with helplessness, but also with embarrassment, because lashing out at one another by the bed of an attempted suicide was simply unthinkable, and making a scene wasn't on either, at least not straight away. József knew that too, but it didn't make the situation any better.

After they had, one by one, expressed their concern, silence fell in the room, because none of them was sure what should happen next. But we are, after all, talking about the late 1950s, and in those days something like a social hierarchy was still respected: wife came before ex-wife who came before lover. And so, after a while, two of the women discreetly, if reluctantly, withdrew, one for ever, the other for at least half an hour, and József Molnár was left alone with his wife.

*1*

IN MY FAMILY people often get to know each other very late, and sometimes not at all. On the other hand, a lot of thinking is done about other family members, particularly when we don't know anything about them or would prefer to know nothing. And stories are told, and you can never be sure whether they're true or not or who could have made them up. Because what other families call their family tree is, in our case, a kind of Sudoku that people have been working on for years, and with lots of rubbings-out, because there's a different result every time. The stories simply won't fit. Some rule each other out, others outdo one another with florid details, and anyway it's too late to check because there's no one left who knows the answer. Because that's the only thing the stories have in common: all their heroes are dead.

This weekend my grandfather József, known as Joschi, would have turned a hundred. My grandfather was a man who lost his wives and children the way other people lose socks or biros. If it wasn't fate that took them away from him, he made sure that he lost them himself. Sadly I never met him. When he died, my mother and Hannah were just a few years older than I am today. I'm sixteen. Hannah and my mother are half-sisters. They were fourteen the first time they saw each other, and since then they've met each other quite often. Hannah is five months younger than my mother. My family has done a lot of thinking on this subject, and there are tons of stories about it.

The idea of turning Joschi's hundredth birthday into a special sort of family reunion was Hannah's, but without my support it would certainly have been scuppered by resistance on my mother's part. One problem was Buchenwald. The other problem was Gabor. In the case of Buchenwald, my mother had understood at last that it was finally time for her to visit the place where her father had been a prisoner. Gabor was a different matter. Gabor is also a child of my grandfather's, although child is a slightly odd term for a sixty-year-old. My mother had always known Gabor, but she was fourteen when she found out he was her half-brother. They hadn't heard from one another for about thirty years. I'm sure it would sound far more exciting if I were to go on to say that we had to dig Gabor out from the Australian outback or some remote weather station in Siberia, but actually we found him in my mother's address book. For over three decades he'd been living about 400 kilometres from us, always in the same house in the same street with the same phone number that my mother put in her diary year after year without ever feeling a desire to phone him up. They had nothing to say to each other, was her explanation, which I found very suspicious if only because there was practically nothing in the world that my mother didn't have something to say about. Hannah was also of the opinion that there was a certain risk involved in inviting Gabor to this reunion, but she insisted on everyone being present, and as it was taken as read that Joschi's first two children had died in Auschwitz, and no one had any names or clues or concrete information about them, Gabor made the gathering complete. Along with me, of course, the only grandchild as far as we knew.

I had offered to ring Gabor because I thought it might be exciting to greet an unknown uncle with the words 'Hi there, this is your niece', but Hannah said it was her business, and she did persuade him to come. She said afterwards it had been hard work. My mother said she was sure he must have demanded money for it, but I don't believe that, particularly since I've never heard her say a single kind word about Gabor. When I asked Hannah about her relationship with Gabor, she told me she'd met him for the first time a few years after Joschi's death, and they simply hadn't been on the same wavelength. Even that I found somehow suspicious. Hannah's the one who's most involved in our family Sudoku, and that she should have been the one to neglect a source of information for several decades struck me as rather unprofessional. It didn't have to be love at first sight. When I said that to her, she laughed and said she would be perfectly willing to change her opinion after all these years, but she'd also have to have a good reason. I have to say, I was gradually becoming very curious about my uncle.

Our plan was to meet on Friday at the station in Weimar to pick Gabor up from the train and then all drive together to the hotel. Buchenwald was scheduled for Saturday, and Sunday was Joschi's birthday, but how exactly we were going to celebrate it no one could really imagine. My suggestion that we name a star after him, or at least an area of high pressure (I'd found out that the chances of one starting with the letter J were good for mid-October), had been mercilessly dashed. If there was a meteorological phenomenon that Joschi could be compared to, my mother said, it was more like a whirlwind. So we left the ceremonial part open and hoped for spontaneous inspiration.

And now we were standing on the draughty platform, my mother and I, waiting for Gabor's train to come in at last. The arrivals board showed a fifteen-minute delay, and the computerized voice from the loudspeaker repeated this information every few minutes and in the end asked us in German for our understanding and thanked us in English for our patience. I thought the English text was somehow nicer, even though I felt neither understanding nor patient. My mother started counting the platforms, out of boredom, I assumed, but then she suddenly asked me if she'd ever told me the story of Joschi's journey on which he had supposedly only taken trains that left from platform 5, no matter where they were going – the main thing was platform 5, only ever platform 5.

'Was that a true story or did he just make it up?' I asked.

'Good question,' my mother replied.

My grandfather was a storyteller, and of course my mother has become one as well. I know most of them, even if I often used to get places and names and times mixed up. The funny thing about these stories is that the ones everyone claims are true sound as if they'd been made up by someone who didn't know anything about storytelling. Sometimes my mother comes up with a new one, but the old, old stories that I grew up with have changed with the course of time. They flourished and got longer and more involved, more ludicrous and more painful, because my mother never tells a story twice in the same way, and no one in the world would ever dare to interrupt her by saying 'I know that one already', unless he was weary of life or stupid or hadn't really been paying attention. The best thing is watching her do it: her eyes gleam, or grow narrow and hard, and her voice sounds full or piercing, and sometimes amused or mocking, and even if my head spins afterwards I know that these stories have found their place somewhere inside me, where they wait for me to summon them up.

I was just wondering if it would be OK to get out my iPod and listen to a bit of music, but at that moment the train suddenly came in, and at the same time I realized how nervous my mother was. Her back was so stiff that mine started hurting too, so I relaxed my muscles and hoped the same thing would happen to her. Not many people got off the train in Weimar. We were around the middle of the platform and had a good view in both directions, and I spotted Gabor first, although I didn't know what he looked like. I only knew pictures that showed him as a grinning twenty-year-old on his moped, and by now he was three times that age. I nudged my mother and pointed to him, and her back stiffened even further, if that was possible, so it had to be him.

'I don't get it,' she whispered. 'He's the spit of Joschi.'

'I think he's the spit of you,' I whispered back, without thinking of the consequences. Obviously it was a stupid remark, particularly since Gabor had a bald patch. The top part of his head peeped out like bare earth from a semi-circle of long grey hair held together by a rubber band at the back. He was wearing jeans and a brown checked shirt and over it a worn brown jacket, and on his considerable nose there rested a pair of aviator sunglasses from the 1970s that looked as if he and they had grown old together. The sunglasses were as thick at the edges as the bottom of a bottle. He looked like a maths teacher. My mother didn't look like a maths teacher. But something about the way he peered along the platform with a frown and squinting eyes was very familiar to me.

'Now I know,' I said. 'You've both got big noses and meerkat faces.'

'Everyone under the age of eighty-one has a face like a meerkat when he's peering for someone on a station platform,' my mother snorted angrily and set off.

Because I thought she was more in need of my support than my company, I lagged about two or three metres behind her. I counted her steps: as she took the fifth one she had to step over a dog lead, and with the ninth one she tripped slightly. With the thirteenth Gabor finally recognized her – which was good for me, because another three steps and she would simply have walked past him and it would have been up to me to greet him. Gabor looked at my mother and blinked nervously behind his thick glasses. He stretched out his hand, but then changed his mind and instead reached behind him to his thin ponytail, as if to check that it was still in the right place. Then he lowered his arm again. He looked scared.

'Hello, Marika,' said Gabor. He pronounced it properly, in the Hungarian way with the stress on the first syllable, and that must have worked in his favour. Most people say Ma-riiii-ka, and it's hard to persuade them not to, because there was once a Hungarian actress who put up with that mistake for a hundred years because she was really deaf from birth and couldn't hear herself singing or anyone else saying her name, or at least that's what Joschi told my mother.

'Hi, Gabor.' They stood facing one another with their arms dangling at their sides and clearly neither one of them had any great desire to touch the other. Either that or they weren't brave enough. When they had last seen each other shortly after Joschi's death, my mother was a punk and Gabor was an arsehole – at least that's what my mother claims. I know enough about punk to know that these two qualities are irreconcilable, and it looked to me as if they wanted to start exactly where they'd left off. Or stop, maybe, because nothing else happened. I could tell by my mother's stiff shoulders that my relaxation spell hadn't worked.

I decided to make myself known, and Gabor, who seemed very pleased with the change, called out when he saw me: 'What – that couldn't be my niece? My goodness, I thought you were still a little girl . . .'

I obligingly shed a few years on the spot. 'Hi, I'm Lily,' I said and held out my hand. His was freezing, and his smile looked as if he'd been practising it in the train, and hadn't quite finished in time even though the train had been so late. His teeth were small and surprisingly white. They probably weren't his own. He smelled of cigarette smoke and maths teacher.

'Hey, I've brought you something,' he said, and started rummaging in his battered olive-green shoulder bag. 'But it hadn't occurred to me that you were almost grown up – oh, here it is.' He took out a brown plush bear. 'This is the hero of our department,' he said proudly. 'He's passed all the tests with flying colours. Maximum traction on all limbs simultaneously, constant pressure, extreme temperatures, even his eyes stayed in right to the end, and God knows you can't say that about his colleagues.'

I admit it, my mouth was really hanging open because I didn't understand a thing, even though I knew I'd grasped all his words correctly. Gabor was holding the bear right in front of my nose in such a way that there was nothing I could do but grab it. Maximum traction on all limbs? Gabor wouldn't have looked half as pleased if he had any idea how obnoxious his words had sounded.

'Could you please repeat that?' my mother said, and pulled a face as if she was a member of PETA or the Humane Society and might give them a call at any minute.

Gabor started to explain, but at that moment Hannah finally came running over, wearing, as ever, a fluttering silk scarf, talking to someone invisible, and plainly late. She was waving and gesticulating and speaking on the phone all at the same time, and when she caught up with us she simply thrust her mobile into a bewildered Gabor's hand and then threw her arms around his neck. I would have loved to have known who was at the other end, and listening in on our reunion. If he – or she – had anything to say on the matter, it was drowned out by Hannah's greeting. 'My darling brother,' she cried in a voice so loud that all the darling brothers in hearing distance probably lost a beat, 'Welcome to the family circle!' Gabor just stood there like a concrete post and let her get on with it, and when I realized that I was holding the bear away from myself in exactly the same way as he was holding Hannah's phone, the giggles that I'd been holding back for so long suddenly came bubbling out of me.

'Have I missed something interesting?' Hannah asked and took the phone back from Gabor, snapped it shut and stuffed it in her handbag, where it immediately started ringing again. It was the theme tune from *Once Upon a Time in the West.* That made me laugh even more, while my mother rolled her eyes, but Hannah was completely unmoved and pulled me to her. For a while I plunged into the wonderful world between Hannah's huge, soft breasts, where I felt even safer for the knowledge that mine would never, ever be that big. As long as Hannah's are, everything's fine. The same is true of her loud voice and her red hair, which looks like exploded wire wool, and feels like it too. For me Hannah isn't so much a tower of strength as a red lifeboat that bobs worryingly up and down but will never capsize.

'Already sorry you came?' Hannah asked, letting me re-emerge, and I shook my head and was about to show her the bear when her phone started wailing again. Hannah took it out, glanced at the display, sighed and turned it off.

It was hard to tell whether she was sighing because of the caller or because she couldn't take the call, but it looked rather romantic. Then she walked over to my mother, who was standing slightly apart with a vertical crease in her forehead that looked like an exclamation mark.

'Don't look so gloomy, big sister,' Hannah said amiably. 'I promise, my phone will be turned off all weekend. And yes, the tune is completely irrelevant. I could just as well have selected a Jewish ringtone. What do you think of "Hava Nagila"?'

'Really?' I asked. 'They have Jewish ringtones for mobiles?'

'With optional Star of David or Menorah as wallpaper,' Hannah replied.

'Then at least your phone would have converted,' my mother said.

'A Jewish mobile's a good start,' Hannah said.

I wanted to ask Gabor what the deal was with that bear, but instead I watched him watching my mother and Hannah hugging. His face was completely expressionless. My mother sometimes says she and Hannah are like Laurel and Hardy, but I think they're more like Holmes and Watson. What Gabor felt as he looked at them both one could only imagine. My guess was sheer horror.

'Shall we go?' Hannah asked. I put the bear, whose supposed abuse had left no visible trace, carefully in my rucksack and followed the others towards the exit.

# 2

WE WENT OUR SEPARATE WAYS immediately after check-
ing into the hotel. Hannah said she had a few urgent calls
to make before she could finally switch off her phone,
Gabor said nothing at all, and even my mother didn't
seem in a particular hurry to get on with the official start
of our memorial weekend. No one asked me, and we
arranged to meet two hours later at the Italian restaurant
right beside our hotel. Gabor's room was next to ours, but
he preferred to go upstairs rather than taking the lift with
us, although of course he didn't put it quite as directly as
that. As we were getting out, we just had time to see him
disappearing into his room. My mother raised her right

eyebrow, which she's very good at doing, but she didn't say anything until she'd closed the door to our room behind her.

'In all the years I've known him, that guy has texted me from dawn till dusk. Why has he stopped talking all of a sudden?'

I couldn't think of an answer, but I don't think she was expecting one.

'At first I really thought that was Joschi standing on the platform. Do you really think we look alike? And careful what you say now.'

There was no chance of backtracking, and she wouldn't have wanted me to do that, so only the collision course was left. 'I think if you put on the same glasses and stood next to him, you wouldn't be able to tell the two of you apart.'

My mother squinted and wobbled her head back and forth. 'Like that, maybe?'

'Exactly like that,' I said. 'Except, of course, you're much prettier than he is.'

'Fine, I'll never ask you again,' said my mother and glanced into the bathroom. What she saw there filled her with great contentment. 'I think I'll have a go in the bath-tub,' she announced as if this was something quite new, when in fact it's something she does every time she spots one somewhere: she lies down in it, for hours. I'm not like that. Bathtubs make me nervous. As soon as I'm in it I wonder what would happen if the tub suddenly cracked underneath me. In my imagination there are heating elements under bathtubs just as there are under a ceramic hob, and I'm sure that someone will invent something like that one day to keep the bathwater hot for longer. Bathtubs aren't good places for me. Other places I'm suspicious about are solariums, MRI scanners, tunnels whose exit you can't see when you drive into them, and space capsules.

While the bathwater was running, we made another couple of important decisions such as who was sleeping on which side of the big double bed and whether I would have unlimited access to the television in the hotel room. We agreed in both cases, and I zapped through the meagre selection of channels for a while and then got Gabor's bear out of the rucksack. It looked like new. On a little label in the stitch in its right ear it said 'Made in China'. I put it on my pillow and wondered where my altar could go in this room, because I had the feeling I might be needing it here. Then I decided to go out. I knocked on the bathroom door, and when there was no answer I knocked again and finally I went in and saw that my mother was still in a state of total immersion. She says she likes it when her ears are under water, because there are sounds and noises that you can't hear in the air, and besides, it's so peaceful down there. With the best will in the world, I can't find vessels of water that might theoretically have elements behind them restful. We've often talked about it, my mother and I, and of course she has wondered whether something might have gone wrong with me during her pregnancy, but neither of us has ever been able to remember anything in particular. It was only after I had, like all the other children, done my 'little seahorse' swimming competition and even fetched three plastic rings up from the bottom of the pool for her sake, that she stopped worrying about me and I stopped screaming when she drifted like a drowned corpse in the bathtub.

'I'm going out,' I said when she had re-emerged.

'What?' she asked, but then she immediately switched back to mother mode. 'We're eating at seven. Have you got your phone?'

'Yep,' I said, and blew her a kiss and left.

I've never been to Weimar before. I'm full of prejudices about East Germany and mental images of places where skinheads in Doc Martins are hanging around all over the place and beating up people like me. Even so, MRI scanners are much worse. My grandmother was in one once; she told me about it, and she said she prayed in there out of sheer loneliness. I could weep today, just thinking about it. I miss her so. My grandmother had been married to Joschi, but when I was born she'd already been living with Karl for a long time, so Karl became my grandfather. They both died last year, one after the other, which was doubtless good for her, but not for us. Other contestants for number one spot in the bad news stakes last year were: my cat was run over; I missed the deadline for the short-story competition at my school; my friend Helene had sex with a boy I was head over heels in love with, which neither of them knew and that somehow made it all the worse; and my father moved out.

This year things had been going far better for me, that much was clear.

To my great relief, instead of Nazis there were only normal people walking about in the street, and the ones who weren't walking were sitting outside the cafés wrapped in blankets, smoking or stretching their necks to catch the last of the October sunlight. I put my iPod headphones in my ears and watched the live broadcast of *Lily in Weimar* while listening to the new Coldplay album. My life as film – I often do that when I'm outside listening to music. Everything I see gets this incredible significance: an empty plastic bag in the branches of a tree, a guy sitting with his laptop on a park bench picking his nose, a woman discreetly trying to adjust her breasts in her bra. I seek out good scenes for good music, because in the end I'm switched to transmit, and everybody's watching me live, maybe even Jan, to whom I've devoted most of my broadcasts recently. With the right soundtrack even the pedestrian precinct in Weimar can look as exciting as Sunset Boulevard in an MTV clip. I'm director, presenter and main character rolled into one, my eyes are the camera, and right in front of me is another one, in case I want to present something, and above all so that Jan can see me.

A young couple came out of a bakery on my right. She took a chocolate éclair out of its wrapper and held it up in front of his nose. He shook his head. She looked at him and, without taking her eyes off him, stuck her finger into the éclair, took it back out and ran her whipped-cream finger along his lips. At first he pulled a surprised face, then started smiling and kissing her. I turned away because I thought it was intrusive to watch other people kissing, but I liked the scene, and I wanted to be the girl and be kissed by Jan. On the opposite side of the street a little boy walked backwards, gesticulating wildly, and after a few yards he tripped over the outstretched leg of a tattooed man with dreadlocks who was sitting on the ground with a little frying-pan in front of him with a few coins in it and a dog beside him. The dog was black and overweight and wearing a Palestinian scarf. On a piece of cardboard resting against the frying pan it read: *I bet you 50 cents you smile when you read this*. The boy cried, the dog barked (silently for me, but with a dramatic musical background), whereupon the man reached into the pan and held a coin out to the child. The boy looked at him with horror and ran away. A bit further off to the left, a woman had got up so clumsily from her seat in the street café and a table had started wobbling menacingly. The man at the next table grabbed one of the cups before it could fall off. She was completely unaware of what was happening. Another everyday hero, who would have gone undiscovered without my keen camera eye.

I zoomed in on him: it was Gabor. He looked right into my camera, and the light of the setting sun was reflected in his Coke-bottle glasses.

I took the headphones out of my ears and turned the music off. Gabor smiled at me. At first I was a bit uncertain because he'd caught me playing, but then I reassured myself with the thought that you couldn't tell that from outside, as long as I wasn't talking out loud.

'Do you want to join me?' Gabor shouted, and it sounded like a serious invitation.

'I'm coming,' I said.

At least he hadn't wrapped himself up in one of those ridiculous blankets, but I must admit that after a while I felt so cold that I took one even though I found it a bit embarrassing. We sat side by side for a long time without saying anything, watching the people in the pedestrian precinct. I stirred my cappuccino until the foam had turned all the way back to milk.

'Have you ever been to Buchenwald, Gabor?' A risky opening, but I was really interested.

'God, no.'

'Me neither,' I said 'Neither has Mum. But Hannah's been there. She says it really gets to you.'

'Exactly,' said Gabor. He took a pack of cigarettes out of his pocket. Of course, those are the people who absolutely have to sit outside in October. The index and middle fingers of his right hand were yellow with nicotine. He lit a cigarette and inhaled deeply.

'I don't need to process the past in that way,' he said. 'And it doesn't help all those dead Jews, either.'

'But you're a Jew, too,' I said.

23

'How do you work that one out?' Gabor's eyes glittered behind his glasses. 'Because my father was supposedly a Jew? You're only deemed to be a Jew if you have a Jewish mother, and none of us has one of those. And anyway I have no idea about the Jewish religion. Why should I be a Jew?'

I didn't understand why he said 'supposedly'. I knew the thing about the German mother already.

'I'm not a Jew,' Gabor repeated emphatically. 'It was all just chance. It doesn't mean anything, do you understand?'

'But it means something to me,' I said. 'I'm glad that I somehow belong.'

'Yes, Lily,' replied Gabor. 'But somehow belonging is only OK if you don't really need it, because you're already at home somewhere else. If you really want to belong, you're not even going to get past the doorman with that "somehow". They'll only let you in if you have a real ticket.'

'You make it sound as if you're well acquainted with doormen,' I said at random.

Gabor laughed. It was a brief, sniggering laugh that seemed to surprise even him, because he listened to it for a while before he answered. 'You bet I am. Whenever I've made it past the doormen, then the doors have always got me.'

I imagined Gabor rattling and shaking the door of a synagogue and not getting it open, but then I realized that he was probably talking about something quite different from being Jewish.

'And where do you belong?' I asked.

'Me?' said Gabor. 'I don't belong anywhere. And you want to write a presentation on Buchenwald, I heard?'

I knew that kind of evasiveness very well – it always happens when people suddenly remember they're talking to a sixteen-year-old. They change the subject, or briefly establish who's the grown-up here and who isn't, and from then on the conversation is on the children's channel.

'Did Hannah tell you that?' I asked to gain some time.

'Yes,' said Gabor. 'Quite honestly, until then I didn't know you existed. That's funny, isn't it?'

In fact I didn't think it was particularly funny, but rather typical of our family. And who could have told him? 'And actually why have you and Hannah and Mum had no contact with each other?'

Gabor took another cigarette. 'I assume the two of them aren't very interested in me.'

'What about you?'

'Oh, you know, eventually there was just no point in me calling,' Gabor replied, and again I sensed that he himself was surprised by what he was saying. 'I had nothing new to report.' With the tip of his cigarette he drew lines in the ash at the bottom of the ashtray. It turned into a flower. 'And anyway I'm not family oriented.' He mixed the ash up with the cigarette, so that it was nothing but dust, and the flower was gone.

'Tibetan monks do that too,' I said.

'They smoke?' Gabor asked irritably.

'They make mandalas out of brightly coloured sand,' I said, and because Gabor went on looking at me uncomprehendingly, I added: 'Mandalas are symmetrical pictures. Everything is built around a central point. The monks often spend weeks and months sitting at a sand mandala like that. And when they've finished, they immediately destroy it again. Or they tip it into the river. Whooooosh.'

'Whooosh,' Gabor repeated. 'Why?'

'Because everything is transient. And even destruction is a sacred act.'

'Destruction as a sacred act,' Gabor said slowly. 'I like that.'

'So what was really up with the bear you brought with you?' I asked.

'Another sacred act,' said Gabor. 'The bear's like a colleague of mine. I work in a lab that tests toys for durability. It's like an MOT for cuddly animals.'

I have to admit, I was relieved, although I myself could have imagined that he did something with toys. 'Cool. And you do all kinds of tests, and the ones that don't break can be sold?'

'Pretty much,' said Gabor, stubbing out his cigarette. 'The bear I brought with me hasn't been tested, of course. These guys always look pretty exhausted afterwards, even if they've passed. But he comes from a family that's getting its certificate. Good genes. A true hero.'

I liked the way he talked about the bear, and I briefly thought about giving him a name, even though I don't like doing things like that, because it's a kind of promise of love that I'm too old for. I'd really have liked to ask Gabor why he had such a funny job, but I couldn't think of anything that wouldn't have sounded importunate. And also I could rely on the fact that sooner or later my mother or Hannah, who wasn't backward in such matters, would ask him the question.

'Shall we make our way back to the hotel? We've a dinner date in half an hour,' Gabor asked, looking as if he wasn't particularly looking forward to our meeting. It had grown dark, and I looked for the man with the dog and the coins in the frying pan. He had gone. Gabor paid. His wallet looked old and worn. When I got up a smell of old man reached my nose, not bad, not strong, but definitely that mixture of tobacco, maths teacher and loneliness.

# 3

WHEN WE GOT BACK TO THE HOTEL, my mother and
Hannah were sitting suitably illuminated on a leather sofa
in the lobby, each holding a glass of sparkling wine, and
quite blatantly involved in a silly flirtation with the waiter
at the hotel bar, whose gelled hair made him look like a
seal, and who was also at least twenty years younger than
both of them. I now expect no other behaviour from
Hannah, but I didn't especially like the fact that my
mother was hugely enjoying herself – even less that Gabor
was watching attentively. Hannah noticed us first, and
waved so hard that her wine glass slopped over, which
provoked a little attack of merriment in my mother, and

finally got our friend Sammy the Seal into top gear. He ran to help with a pile of paper napkins, enough to dry out half the foyer, but then didn't dare go into action himself, instead placing the napkins on the arm of the sofa next to Hannah so clumsily that they immediately fell down again.

'Can I offer you something to drink as well, Miss?' he asked me, and I knew that under normal circumstances this guy would never have been so formal, or else he'd have studiously ignored me, so I put as much contempt into my voice as possible when I said, 'No, thanks.' Gabor also declined his offer.

'Where have you been?' my mother wanted to know.

'Outside in a café,' I said, and slumped into an armchair.

'I'll be back in a quarter of an hour,' said Gabor and fled towards the stairs. He wasn't even out of range when Holmes and Watson caught me in their claws.

'Did you have a chance to talk to each other?' (Hannah)

'Was he friendly with you?' (my mother)

'Did he talk about himself?' (Hannah)

'Did he say anything about his relationship with Joschi?' (my mother)

I admit, I like being the centre of attention, especially when I have information that other people want, so at first I pretended I had to make an enormous effort even to remember where and with whom I had spent the last hour.

'I know how to delete all the songs on your iPod,' my mother said pleasantly.

'And don't imagine your life will be any nicer when I get custody of you,' Hannah said, just as courteously.

'All right,' I said. 'He told me—'

In that moment my phone started to ring.

'That's not fair,' Hannah protested. 'I had to turn mine off.'

'Yours will stay off too,' said my mother.

I retreated to the other end of the lobby, where the others couldn't hear me. It was my father.

'Hi there, Tigerlily,' he said. 'Good time?'

'Not really,' I said. 'We're still in the hotel and we're about to go and eat.'

'What's the mood like?'

'It's fine.'

'I just wanted to tell you I'll be thinking about you tomorrow. About all of you,' he added quickly, and I noticed that he really wanted to say 'you and Mum', and then thought better of it. 'I'm sure it'll be an important day for you.'

'I think so too,' I said. 'Are you at Nora and Paul's?'

'No, I'm at my flat,' he said.

'Kiss Paul from me.'

'Will do,' said my father. 'Hey, Tigerlily, take care. I love you.'

'Love you too.'


Apart from its lack of clarity, our family story has one further quality: it likes to repeat itself. My grandfather had five children by completely different women, and my father who, unlike us, can trace his ancestors back to the Middle Ages, and isn't even related to Joschi, just continued this tradition and had his second child with Nora, the old flame of his youth, who had just planned to pop by for a moment. At least I didn't have to wait for fourteen years until I met my brother Paul, and I loved him from the first minute. But Paul's existence also made it impossible for me to go on hating my father, which no one had asked me to do anyway, least of all my mother. But perhaps it had also been precisely that – the almost unbearable fairness with which she tried to separate her own concerns from mine – that had made me hate him of my own free will in the first place – on a trial basis, so to speak. It didn't suit me, and the first time I held Paul in my arms, the feeling that something had gone terribly wrong in my life suddenly stopped.

My father and Nora hadn't been a couple for ages, and as far as I know they never really were one. Even so, I didn't manage to fill my mother with enthusiasm for the thought of my father moving back in with us. She said she didn't feel like copying the life of her own mother, who in spite of seventeen long years by Joschi's side had never managed to forgive him Hannah's existence. And she herself, my mother stressed, was not concerned with forgiveness but with her decision to step off the hamster wheel of this miserable family history, in which women were impregnated and lies told without interruption. What surprised me was that she used the term 'step off the hamster wheel', because as a child my mother had owned a hamster, which bore the name of Roger and was renowned for his spectacular escapes. Roger liked tearing the cotton out of his bed at night, and stuffing it under the running-wheel, so that he could climb up the outside of the jammed wheel and flee through a gap in the roof of the cage that my negligent mother seldom closed properly. The gapingly empty cave in the morning, with its specially manipulated wheel, had been a manifesto of the triumphant small mammal, my mother said, but also testimony to his borderline mental deficiency, because right next to the cage stood a big bag of hamster feed, into which the idiot would unfailingly plunge immediately after his act of liberation. So he would be found in the morning, almost incapable of motion, in the food bag, his cheek pouches as plump as car tyres, and the outlines of the individual corns of maize and sunflowers clearly discernible from his outside. He had probably opted for food over freedom on every occasion – that was my mother's interpretation of his behaviour – but I always thought this hamster tale was a metaphor for something much bigger, for example that you could find paradise even in a bag, as long as it was hard enough to get there.

I went back to the sofa. Hannah had clearly managed to wangle yet another special permission, and was reading a text message on her phone with a transfigured smile. 'Do you need to go back up to the room?' my mother asked, raising an eyebrow, and I answered in thought-language, it was Dad, and he's thinking about us, but at normal volume I said, 'No, I've got everything I need,' and at that moment it wasn't even a lie.

'Lucky thing,' said Hannah, turning her phone back off.

Only a few minutes after me, Gabor turned up in a red shirt that looked very old-fashioned and reminded me of a Tibetan monk, and suddenly he seemed wildly determined to make the very best of this evening and perhaps even of the whole weekend. He gallantly held out his right hand to Hannah, to help her from the leather sofa, and then he briefly pressed my arm before telling my mother how glad he was that she had left her punk phase behind and had instead brought up a wonderful daughter, which must actually have got him one if not two bonus points.

'Anarchy, no mercy for the rich,' said my mother, but you could see that she was relaxing a little.

Hannah graciously waved goodbye to Sammy after signing the bill, and linked arms with me. 'Don't say a thing,' she whispered. 'Particularly if you were going to say he looks like shit and he's too young for me anyway.'

'He looks great,' I said. 'He's probably fallen in love with you.'

'I think so,' said Hannah. 'And I've met someone, by the way.'

When Hannah 'met someone' it usually meant that the Jewish dating club had selected a new partner for her on the basis of her profile. It also meant that the next few days and weeks were full of stories about various Aris, Jaakovs,

Joels or Gils who sounded more or less exciting and always trickled away in the sand again. That seemed to matter astonishingly little to Hannah, just as little as it curbed her enthusiasm and confidence that she would one day emigrate to Israel with the right man by her side. When I was younger, I firmly expected that one day I would open the mailbox and find a card from Haifa or Tel Aviv with her new address. Once she had almost succeeded, she was with an Eli from Eilat and had already completed the fifth two-hour class of a crash course in Hebrew, but then it turned out that Eli's family had serious concerns about a relationship with a shiksa from Germany, and because the family had quite a lot of money that concern soon took hold of Eilat Eli as well, and that was that. I think Hannah was more troubled than usual about this particular affair, because it hadn't been about Hannah herself but about her questionable origins as a Jew on her father's side – a *Vaterjüdin*. I thought this word was an insult when I first heard it, but Hannah explained to me that it was merely a term to describe the children of Jewish fathers and non-Jewish mothers. *Vaterjuden*, she said, could claim Israeli citizenship, but if they wanted to be real Jews, they first had to convert, with everything that entailed. I'm pretty sure that there was hardly anything in her life that pissed Hannah off as much as this fact.

'What's his name?' I asked.

'Edgar,' she replied.

'Edgar? Is he not Jewish?'

'No, he is,' said Hannah. 'No idea how he ended up with that first name.'

I thought a Jew called Edgar would suit our family perfectly, but it was too early for comments like that, particularly since it was much more likely that none of us would ever set eyes on Edgar.

'Gabor's nice,' I said instead. 'He's a toy tester, and he blows up teddy-bears.'

'Wow,' said Hannah. 'What an interesting job. I didn't even know he had one.'

The Italian restaurant was called Da Enzo and when we got there it was completely empty apart from one solitary guest in the window. Somewhere in the background a football match was being broadcast with an Italian commentary, and a bad-tempered middle-aged woman rattled through the 'specialities of the day that aren't on the menu' in a strong Saxon accent. Her hair was in a beehive and she had metallic-blue eyelids. Gabor stared at her wide-eyed from behind his aviator glasses, as if he expected her to shed her arms or legs or go up in flames at any moment. When she at last withdrew, he exhaled audibly.

'Whatever you think, I reckon she did her job very well,' said Hannah.

'Was that Mrs Enzo?' I asked.

'No,' said my mother. 'I reckon she's called Peggy and she helps out on Fridays because it's always packed to the gills in here.'

'Am I right in thinking that she said something about "kosher"?' Hannah asked.

'Not in a million years,' said my mother. 'She said "coccio". Or tried to. It's a fish, but don't ask me which one.'

'I'll have a pizza Margherita and a mineral water,' I said, and snapped the menu shut.

'Me too,' said Gabor with relief.

Peggy took our orders with a blank expression, and came back surprisingly quickly with our drinks.

Hannah raised her glass. 'To the family,' she said, and that was probably supposed to mark the official start of our weekend together.

'To the family,' the rest of us replied, which sounded a bit silly with us all speaking at once, and suddenly everyone was embarrassed, each in their own way. Gabor took out a checked handkerchief and started cleaning his glasses, which gave me my first opportunity to see his eyes properly. They were green or greenish-brown and had big, heavy bags under them. Hannah inspected her red wine and fished out an invisible bit of cork. I tried to remember how to fold a lotus blossom out of a paper napkin, but unfortunately I couldn't even remember the first step. And my mother did what she often does in such situations: she took the bull by the horns.

'And of course to our father,' she said. 'Jószef Molnár, King of Hearts and the Ace up the Sleeve, the Jack of All Parades ...'

'I hope you never find yourself in the situation of having to give a real speech about him,' Hannah said.

'Oh, that I'd like to hear,' said Gabor.

'This one *is* real,' said my mother. 'But there's much more, that's true.'

Peggy brought the salad. A family with three small children came into the restaurant. They made a horrific racket.

'But what I'd love to know,' said Gabor, pouring himself some mineral water, 'is what you really think – about our father.'

'You start,' said Hannah with her mouth full.

'All right, then,' Gabor replied. 'At the risk of repeating myself, I thought our father was a bit of a dick.'

'You've repeated yourself,' said my mother. 'It may be just a few decades since the last time, but who cares. And apart from that?'

'I could go into greater detail.'

'Off you go,' said Hannah.

'As long as it's from sixteen onwards,' added my mother.

'Stories about fathers mostly start at six,' I said.

Peggy brought our meals. Gabor looked as if he'd rather have had an ashtray, but he had spoken up of his own free will, and now it was time for his story.

# 4

'BASICALLY you can sum it up in a few sentences,' said Gabor and picked a basil leaf off his pizza. 'Instead of a speech, years ago I thought up an inscription for his gravestone: He loved women, he had no idea about contraception, he lied his head off, and when things got tough he pissed off.'

'Rather unusual in Jewish cemeteries,' said Hannah, energetically twirling the pepper mill.

'Don't you act so jaded,' said Gabor. 'I think even you must have had your weak moments every now and again, when you wished he'd stayed with you.'

'Of course I had,' Hannah replied. 'But these days I don't go round wailing about it.'

'You did go through at least five therapists,' my mother observed.

'Six,' Hannah corrected her. 'Do you remember what Dr Hirschfeld said, Marika? "Most of us are drowning in a sea of pain. Learn to swim, Frau Wichmann!"'

Gabor looked annoyed. 'I'm not going round wailing. But neither do I plan to prettify the past. I had the dubious fortune of having two arseholes for fathers. One was called Alfred, and the other was called Joschi. And quite honestly I have no idea what I'm actually supposed to be celebrating this weekend.'

I didn't know that much about Gabor and his family history, but the few things I was aware of sounded like a fairytale that hadn't been thought out properly. My mother says Gabor was incredibly unlucky in his childhood, but the decision to become a money-grubbing jerk had in the end been entirely his own. My mother can be ruthless about that kind of thing.

If I've remembered this correctly, Gabor's mother Louise and my grandfather met in Germany shortly after the war. At the time Louise was still married to Alfred, but Alfred had been caught napping by the Red Army along with his Panzer Division, with which he had been fighting in Hungary of all places, and since then had been declared missing. Whether or not Louise was very sad about this history doesn't matter. At any rate Joschi and Louise fell in love, and so that they could be married they had Alfred declared dead. Late in 1947 Gabor was born.

And about two years later – surprise! – there, all of a sudden, was Alfred standing at the front door.

When I imagine this scene, it's always Joschi who goes to open the door with Gabor in his arms. How can I help you, he says to the strange man, but the stranger doesn't reply, he just stares at Joschi, and just as he realizes who's standing in front of him Joschi drops Gabor in shock. My mother says that mightn't even be that wide of the mark, at least symbolically, because shortly after Alfred's return from his prisoner-of-war camp the three of them reached a rather odd compromise: Alfred got Louise back, with Gabor thrown in. Joschi walked away empty-handed, but remained a friend of the family as long as he lived. My mother would later become Louise's god-daughter and spend most of her holidays at her house. Louise, my mother says, was an impressive woman with red-painted fingernails, jangling gold bracelets and blood-red lipstick on her mouth. If she happened not to be smoking or playing Patience, she was either swearing like a trooper or off in hysterical crying jags. As a child, my mother wanted to be Louise more than anything else. Luckily she had second thoughts.

'One thing I've always wanted to ask you,' Hannah said to Gabor. 'Can you actually remember anything from the time before Alfred came back?'

'Oh, please, I was two years old at the time,' said Gabor, and started pushing his pizza back and forth on the plate with the tip of his knife. 'I hadn't the faintest idea. There's quite a long walk with Joschi that I still remember, and that happened after I'd been caught stealing at school. He was going on about how children should be grateful that they had a nice, warm bed and a roof over their head. I hadn't a clue what the whole thing had to do with him, but I was glad that I didn't have to do that bloody awful walk with Alfred.'

Alfred. From all I've heard about him he must have been some kind of child-eating monster. After he came home he embarked on a dazzling career as managing director of a factory making artificial limbs, he was on the board of a bank and had a chauffeur, a villa, a yacht and a problem with the booze. It was better to keep out of his way when he was drunk. And when he wasn't. In spite of this, Louise seemed to get on reasonably well with him, but then on the other hand there were all those smart receptions and cocktail parties and business trips to far-away countries, to which Alfred exported his artificial limbs. Louise had had precisely the right instinct about her husband's final choice, my mother says, but for the sake of fairness one would have to add that she never stopped inviting Joschi to her house and later Joschi and Lotte and, later still, Joschi, Lotte and my mother. That was probably her way of keeping the family together. Why Gabor was, from his tenth year onwards, packed off to boarding schools from which he absconded with increasing regularity, it is not so easy to say. Hannah thinks that in those days it was all part of being a young lad from a good family.

'How did they actually tell you?' my mother asked. 'Or did you go snuffling around in living-room cupboards like Hannah and me?'

'Oh no, I got the classic for my eighteenth birthday,' Gabor replied and started talking in an affectedly distorted voice. 'Gabor darling, Joschi and I have something important to tell you, now that you're a grown-up man.'

'Was Alfred there too?' my mother interrupted.

'No,' said Gabor, now speaking in his normal voice again. 'Just Joschi and Louise. Joschi didn't utter a word and smoked one cigarette after another while Louise tried to present me with a tragic love story that had played out among the ruins of post-war Germany. And then, at the end, noble renunciation on the one hand and generous adoption of wife and bastard child on the other. I could have puked.'

'Now you're the one acting jaded,' said Hannah.

'No, I'm not,' Gabor retorted. 'I really couldn't have cared less. It explained why Alfred had treated me like a failure all my life, but it didn't change anything else at all. They shouldn't have told me. Or do you think Joschi subsequently gave free rein to his paternal feelings?'

'OK but I still don't understand why you call Joschi a dick,' said Hannah. 'Perhaps they'd agreed that he could under no circumstances get involved in your upbringing. Did you know about Joschi's Jewish background at the time, and the story of his wife and children in Auschwitz?'

Gabor gave his pizza a shove that nearly pushed it over the edge of the plate. 'Of course I knew that. Louise hardly ever missed an opportunity to remind me what a terrible fate Joschi had had to endure. I kept wanting to ask him why, in that case, he'd been so keen to get rid of his second son as well, but somehow I never got round to it.'

'I could give you Dr Hirschfeld's address,' Hannah suggested. 'Herschel Hirschfeld. He's a specialist in second-generation victims.'

Gabor looked as if he was about to reply, but then he changed his mind. By now the topping on his pizza had shrunk in on itself, and reminded me of that Bronze Age relic the Nebra sky disc, which must have come from somewhere hereabouts. In my family, eating and telling stories are usually one and the same thing – as are, incidentally, eating and listening – but Gabor had only moved his pizza around while he talked. Now he, my mother and Hannah were staring as if hypnotized at the landscape on his plate, as if that place were something like their shared home, and instead I looked at their faces and tried again to find similarities. The only one I could discover was their pale skin, inherited from Joschi, who was supposed always to have claimed that so much blue blood flowed in his veins that you could see it shimmering through. If someone has a complexion like that, you buy it without question every time they call in sick. I know that from my own experience. It suited Hannah best because of her red hair, while it just made Gabor look old

44

and unhealthy, and made my mother look tired as she almost always was. Her nose and Gabor's were, size apart, actually almost identical, but with the best will in the world I could see no other common features. Where Hannah was round and red and expansive, my mother was thin and dark and straight. It would hardly have occurred to anyone seeing them sitting at a table together that they had the same father.

I wondered what Joschi would say if he could see me and his three children right now, and suddenly I wasn't so sure if he'd be at all pleased that those three had finally come together and were exchanging their stories.

Gabor cleared his throat. 'I'm off for a smoke,' he said and got up.

My mother watched after him as he walked past the counter, ignoring Peggy, whom he very nearly bumped into. 'I'm off too,' she said, picked up her bag from the arm of the chair and followed him.

'Does she still do it?' Hannah asked me, snapping her mobile shut one-handed with skilful brio.

'I think so,' I answered, but I actually had no idea how often my mother still smoked cigarettes these days. What I did know, though, was that since the wild days of her youth she still sometimes smoked dope. She never hid it from me. The grass that lies around in our flat in bags or little tins has been lying around there since as long as I can remember, like tampons, change or aspirins. To get it out of the way: yes, I've tried it too; and no, it didn't happen in her presence, and neither was it any of her business that I smoked. And I haven't made my final decision, but for the time being it's not my thing. It is hers, as she likes to stress. When my mother's stoned, she puts on wonderful music and tells her best stories. I like that about her. It doesn't work for me.

'We still don't know why Gabor blows up cuddly toys,' I say.

'With a life story like that you could actually be grateful that he doesn't blow quite different things sky-high,' said Hannah and listened to the messages in her mailbox, while I tried to imagine Gabor as a Palestinian suicide bomber.

Peggy, who had stayed in the background for quite long enough, arrived to clear away our plates.

'Didn't he like it?' she asked when she saw Gabor's pizza.

'Your food was delicious, but we had so much to talk about,' Hannah replied, and Peggy nodded sympathetically and offered to heat up the pizza in the microwave again.

'That would be incredibly kind of you,' said Hannah.

'Now you've won her heart,' I said when Peggy had disappeared with a stack of plates and an unexpected smile.

'You should have seen your grandfather,' said Hannah. 'He wouldn't just have had Peggy's phone number in his pocket, he'd have had her bank details as well.'

'And she'd have invited him round to her parents' house for coffee on Sunday,' I added.

'The next day she'd have christened her budgerigar "Joschi",' said Hannah, looking lovingly at the display on her phone. 'And then two weeks later he'd have flown away when she was cleaning his cage. Very sad.'

'Just a moment's inattention. He'd never have come back.'

'But he'd have left her a message. He'd have pooped a heart in the sand on the bottom of the cage first.'

We're a family of storytellers, as I said before.

When my mother and Gabor came back to the table, they didn't smell good, but they did look distinctly more relaxed than before.

'The interesting details that suddenly crop up,' my mother said with satisfaction. 'Gabor was just telling me how shocked he had been when he realized I must be his half-sister.'

'You were still curbing your own enthusiasm at this point, were you?' asked Hannah. 'You always described our brother as a rich, vain ninny.'

'You were just using your phone, telltale,' said my mother. 'I saw it quite clearly as I came in.'

'And what did you think the first time you saw Hannah?' I asked Gabor.

Hannah and Gabor looked at each other.

'Lily, our meeting was a disaster,' said Hannah. 'He

hadn't expected an overweight sister, and I hadn't expected a bald brother.'

'That's not true at all,' Gabor cried, outraged. 'I thought you were great.'

'And?' asked Hannah, looking irritated for a moment.

'I thought you were really great,' Gabor said again.

'And I thought you were really peculiar,' said Hannah.

Peggy appeared at our table and served Gabor his reheated pizza with a genuinely regal gesture. 'I put extra mozzarella on it,' she said proudly. Gabor, dumbfounded, looked at the pizza and then at Peggy. He looked like a man whose hat is always being brought back to him, even though he's actually trying discreetly to get rid of it.

'But I didn't even—' he began.

'It's fine,' Hannah said quickly. 'Leave it here, we'll eat it up.'

Peggy withdrew, stony-faced. She was never going to call her budgie Gabor, that much was certain.

Silence fell for a moment. The family with the children had left long ago, the television was off, and apart from the man in the window, who was staring sullenly at his half-full beer, we were the only diners. Peggy stood behind the counter, noisily rinsing glasses. She sounded hurt.

'I still have quite a clear memory of our meeting, even though it's more than twenty-five years ago now,' said Hannah to Gabor. 'Joschi had already been dead for a few years, and your mother had just died of cancer. You told me Alfred had drunk away his managing director's job along with his boat, but at least the house was still standing, and there was enough left over from his generous financial settlement. Actually you just had to wait until Alfred's liver packed in once and for all, and then you'd have enough funds not to have to work until the end of your days. You worked it out for me quite precisely.'

'OK, it's like this . . . ' Gabor began. 'I'd just come back from my first trip to Israel. When I tried to tell you about it, you stalled me by saying I had no business coming to see you with my Jewish routine.'

'Hannah, for heaven's sake,' my mother said. 'You didn't try to show him those pictures of you dancing at the kibbutz with that Hora group of yours?'

'What pictures?' I asked.

'Very bad pictures, Lily,' said my mother.

'I didn't even get round to showing them,' Hannah said regretfully. 'And anyway, after that meeting it was pretty clear to me that you and I didn't have much in common, Gabor. You called me two or three times after that, but I didn't want to meet up again, and you told me I was as arrogant a cow as Marika.'

'My goodness, yes,' said Gabor, looking down at his hands.

'Arrogant cow? Me?' asked my mother. 'How right you were. But not our Hannah. Hannah was always good.'

'Luckily I met you just in time, Marika,' Hannah said contentedly. 'You drove my goodness out of me. And

49

besides, you also managed to stop me joining the Israeli army.'

'That was quite easy,' my mother replied. 'I just had to tell you they did a lot of sport, and that did it.'

'Gabor, calm down,' said Hannah. 'I no longer care how stupidly you behaved back then. Did you at least sort out your money situation?'

Gabor laughed his sniggering laugh. 'Of course not,' he said. 'In that respect I'm entirely my father's son.'

We all knew which father he meant.

# 5

MY MOTHER SAYS Joschi had an incredible talent for improvisation and, what was more, a great gift for sugar-coating failure, which stood him in very good stead because unfortunately he had a wretched instinct for business deals of any kind. Among the many myths that surround his character is the groundbreaking discovery that he is supposed to have revolutionized the brewing process of the electric coffee machine. It's typical of our family that no one can say what sort of invention it could possibly have been. On the other hand, everyone is able to say how Joschi hawked it in a weak moment for a ridiculous sum of money. Sometimes there is even talk of a game of poker,

which he survived only by staking his invention. I know
too little about poker to be able to say whether you could
actually save your skin like that, but my mother says
the list of unusual things that Joschi is supposed to have
gambled away is so long that she considers a patent for
some spare parts for coffee machines entirely within the
realms of possibility.

Where the story of the boxing match is concerned, however, everyone agrees that it must have occurred more or
less as stated, even though it has already passed through
many different memories and accrued a few interesting
details along the way. It takes place in 1949, and so at the
time when he was still married to Louise. That summer my
grandfather had been given a copper-bottomed tip for
making a great deal of money without having to make the
slightest effort. Boxing matches were in demand again,
people said, and my grandfather thought it all too under-
standable for people to want to see someone getting
punched in the face after all those difficult years. So Joschi
decided to become a boxing impresario, and earn himself a
fortune. It wasn't the first of his crazy business ideas, and it
wouldn't be the last, but it was the only one that he put into
effect in grand style.

Joschi rented a gym, the extension, miraculously pre-
served, of a primary school far away on the edge of town,
whose main building had been destroyed in the war and
never reconstructed. He persuaded a handful of friends
and acquaintances to join in with him, and together they

cobbled together a platform for the boxing ring, and in the end they even had enough money left over for a few benches. The high-profile guests were to sit right at the front, and it was there that Joschi put the chairs that he had discovered in a side room. They were intended for five- or six-year-olds but they did have seat-backs, which my grandfather considered more important than the height of the seat. 'Money will pour in, if this is successful. This business will be a success, I can smell it already,' he told his people. In point of fact the gym smelt of sweaty feet and medicine balls, but he took that as a good omen. The hall would hold a good 300 people, including the chairs at the front, and with tickets at fifty pfennigs or even a mark there was bound to be something left over. Joschi took on two promising amateur boxers, one from Wietzendorf and the other from Gifhorn, and it only emerged that they were more or less distantly related to one another later on, when it was too late. Joschi had flyers printed and per-suaded a pub landlord friend to provide a refreshments trolley.

An audience of thirty-six turned up for the Wedemeyer–Frieling fight, about half of whom had free tickets thanks to their connections with the impresario. Given the small number of spectators, the amateur boxer from Gifhorn refused even to lift his fist, let alone to put on his gloves, so his colleague from Wietzendorf had to pull out as well, even though he would really have liked to have decked his opponent whether the spectators had been present or not.

But that was down to the fact that the inhabitants of Wiet-zendorf and Gifhorn had been enemies for generations, and the fact that they were related only made things worse. The tiny audience jeered and demanded their money back, especially the ones with free tickets, and Joschi had his hands full calming down the furious people, and didn't get home until about seven in the morning, long after the sun had risen. Louise was already waiting by the sitting room window, and took a photograph of her returning hero, still unaware whether a victor or a loser was standing in the street, or that only a few months later yet another surprise arrival would be knocking at her door. But this photograph would become famous in our family: Joschi, arms raised in the air, casting a shadow on the cobbled street several times longer than the man himself.

Later, Joschi preferred to tell the story by starting at the end: that in the event of a fire breaking out in the packed gymnasium he would have been capable, in an exemplary fashion and with no bloodshed, of organizing the evacuation of 300 people who had all thoroughly enjoyed themselves. Sadly, such talents didn't bring in the money, and still don't. People who can successfully empty arenas, but can't fill them, have no future as impresarios, let alone making themselves filthy rich, and with that realization Joschi's career in the field of event management ended as quickly as it had begun.

*

My mother must have had that very story in mind when, after a short pause, she asked Gabor, 'Did you ever try your hand as an event manager?'

Gabor looked confused for a moment, but then he worked out what she was referring to.

'Good God, no,' he said and shook his head. 'I've never been interested in gambling and business. You can always just spend your money. You'll get rid of it all sooner or later.' He seemed to be wondering whether or not to go into his financial situation in greater detail. 'But I've still got the house,' he said after a moment. 'Part of it is rented out, and I live down in the basement.'

My mother and Hannah demonstrated an unfamiliar sense of tact and didn't probe any further, for which I was very grateful. That Gabor had, in one way or another, turned from a money-grubbing jerk into a maths teacher was clearly apparent. And there was something else that I urgently needed to know.

'What was that story you were telling about the kibbutz? Did you really dance the Hora?' I knew that the Hora had something to do with Israeli folk music, but the idea of Hannah dancing in a circle was beyond even my imagination.

'With swaying skirts, my dear,' said Hannah. 'I spent a few weeks in a kibbutz in En Gedi – it was 1982. En Gedi is an oasis on the Dead Sea. There's desert all around, but light-skinned princesses like us don't get sunburned there, because it's the lowest point on earth.'

'I'd guess it really was a low point,' said my mother.

'And I was in love with Yoram,' Hannah continued, unperturbed. 'Yoram was the leader of the Hora group in the kibbutz. His cousin Avi had just won second place for Israel in the Eurovision Song Contest. After Nicole, singing "A Little Peace".'

My mother looked as if she was going to throw up.

'And?' Where love stories are concerned, I can even put up with some bad music.

'And nothing,' Hannah sighed. 'Yoram was wild about me, but he couldn't say no. In the end a Norwegian caught his eye. And she was a much worse dancer than me.'

'Her name wasn't Nicole, was it?' my mother asked.

'Her name was Ramborg. I thought that was very appropriate.' Hannah winked at me. 'I'll show you the pictures next time you visit.'

'My goodness, you don't leave anything out, do you?'

'How am I supposed to take that?' Hannah shot back.

'I mean . . . are you actually interested in anything else at all apart from Jewishness?'

'What did you have in mind?' Hannah leant over the table and picked up her glass.

'Red wine? Good food? Music? Literature? Films? Sex?'

'I'm sorry,' said Gabor, embarrassed. 'I didn't mean to tread on anyone's toes.'

I kept an eye out for Peggy. I couldn't see her anywhere. The man at the window and his beer had disappeared too.

They'd probably have knocked off for the night long ago if we hadn't still been sitting there. Peggy was probably crouching in the kitchen next to the microwave, hating us. It was shortly after ten.

'I wouldn't mind if we did tread on each other's toes,' said my mother.

'But not here,' said Hannah. 'Unless you want them to heat this thing up for a third time, Gabor.'

'No thanks,' Gabor replied, after considering his pizza from all sides one last time, with a frown on his face. That was exactly, it seemed to me, how he would have looked at one of his lab testees if they'd given up the ghost prematurely.

'What on earth gave you the idea of becoming a toy-tester?' If no one else seemed to be interested, I would have to find out the answer myself.

'Oh, that's easy,' said Gabor. 'I more or less fell into it by chance. At first I was just a sort of assistant and set up everything for the tests. And then I took it all back down again and cleared it away. Now I run the tests themselves. We mostly test toys from China.'

I must say, I was a bit disappointed, because by now I'd come up with a great explanation for Gabor's choice of profession, involving a half-dead infant and a swallowed teddy-bear eye, which had unleashed in him the burning desire to prevent such accidents henceforward. Gabor, on the other hand, seemed to trace most things in his life back to chance.

'Great job,' said my mother, and Gabor looked at her again with his laboratory expression, probably to work out whether she was serious or not. The result seemed to reassure him.

Peggy, who had noticed that we were thinking of leaving, appeared out of nowhere and took our money as passionlessly as she had taken our order. Not even our tip brought a smile, but on the other hand a fresh love bite had appeared on her neck, about three inches above her right collarbone. I knew my mother and Hannah had spotted it as well. I wondered whether there was a cook somewhere out the back, called Giuseppe or perhaps only Kevin, and whether Peggy had gone on hating us while he was giving her the love bite. I said to myself that some stories go missing because they aren't thought through or told all the way to the end, but that luckily new ones always appear in their place. Then we went outside together.

Outside the air had turned surprisingly mild, almost like a spring evening. My mother suggested going for a little stroll, but Hannah was violently opposed to the idea and said we could happily tread on each other's toes a bit more in the hotel bar. Gabor didn't seem to care, as long as we stayed outside long enough for him to smoke a cigarette. I wasn't especially thrilled by the prospect of having to watch Sammy the Seal trying to get off with my mother and Hannah again, but luckily the bar was so full that special treatment was out of the question. This time there was no more than a yearning glance as he handed them the drinks menus, and a warning one in my direction, which was probably supposed to mean that a superstud like Sammy could spot an under-age girl a mile away instantly and would never pour them an alcoholic drink even if they were accompanied by a parent or legal guardian. I didn't order anything, which seemed to annoy him.

'I'd like to return to the question that Gabor asked at the start of the evening,' said Hannah, and when she saw my mother's questioning face, she added: 'What we think of our father.'

'Hannah, it's late,' my mother said.

'But it's never too late where my childhood's concerned.'

I know the story of Hannah, her mother and Joschi very well, and I think it explains a lot when it comes to understanding Hannah a bit better. At least Gabor looked as if a few explanations wouldn't hurt, and Hannah looked very determined to let him have them. I looked around and established that I didn't like this bar. Too many people in too small a space, and piano music in the background that wouldn't have been out of place in a spa retreat. I'm surprised my mother had nothing to say on the matter.

In spite of the crush, Sammy brought the drinks to our table very quickly, and ostentatiously set a little bowl of nuts down in front of my nose, with a neon-yellow lollipop sticking out of it. That was the point when I started wondering whether I shouldn't really leave the three of them alone with Hannah's childhood. I made my decision even before Sammy had got back to the bar, where he knocked a full cocktail glass with his elbow and tipped it into the lap of a middle-aged woman. It was the perfect cue. I said goodnight to the others and disappeared as quickly as I could. Children can get away with things like that.

# 6

THAT NIGHT I DREAMED ABOUT my grandmother Lotte. We were sitting at her house, at her kitchen table, and on her lap there lay a tabby cat that I had never seen before, and I knew all my grandmother's cats. 'Joschi brought it,' she said and tenderly stroked the cat's fur. 'Just imagine, he has one big poker win, and of all things he brings me a cat. When we've got so many.' I didn't like the cat, it was too big and too fat for my liking, and I asked, 'Where's Grandpa?' meaning Karl. 'Grandpa?' Lotte repeated. 'First take a look in the fridge, where I've got something nice for you today.' That had been one of her standard openings, and I loved the surprises that waited for me there:

puddings, cream desserts, rice puddings, all the things that are always in your grandparents' fridges and never in the fridge at home. I enthusiastically opened the door, but in the fridge there were no delicious sweets, just Joschi. He wasn't much bigger than the cat in Lotte's lap. He was wearing a red shirt and looked at me reproachfully, but he didn't say a word.

'It's high time you got to know your grandfather at last,' Lotte called to me from the kitchen table. 'I've saved him for you specially.' In that case she must have put him in a long time before I was born, I thought, and then I suddenly got terrified that this little Joschi would open his mouth and say something to me, possibly in a squeaky voice, so I slammed the fridge door shut again. 'Why are you doing that?' my grandmother asked, surprised. 'Your grandfather would like to talk to you.' But that was exactly what I didn't want, and I ran out of the door, past my mother, who was digging a hole in the front garden with my father and Gabor ('For Joschi!' she cried excitedly after me), I ran past my grandpa, who was coming towards me on his bicycle, and also wearing a red shirt, I ran and ran and ran, until at last I woke up.

Not exactly the kind of dream that strengthens you for a visit to a former concentration camp, I thought. But would any other kind have been better? I had no idea what would await me in Buchenwald, but I was afraid I'd got off lightly with my dream. My mother's side of the bed was abandoned and empty, but I'd expected that. My mother has a bath or finishes a design or reads or listens to music, but she doesn't sleep, and if she does, she does it secretly. I have a few memories of creeping into my parents' bed on Sunday morning and my mother still being asleep or at least pretending to be asleep, but later, when I was bigger, she was already up, like the hare and the tortoise, except she said, 'I'm awake already', or sometimes 'I'm still awake'. I went to the bathroom, but the tub was dry and empty, which meant that she must already have been up and about. It was a gloomy autumn day outside. It was just before eight, and I knew our family outing wouldn't begin before eleven o'clock, so I decided that this was a good time to meditate.

You can meditate anywhere, Jan says, at the bus stop, by the till in the supermarket and even on the toilet, but you have to have a bit of practice to do that. He has. I don't. When I found out a few months ago that Jan was a Buddhist, of course I thought Buddhism was brilliant, but only because I thought Jan was brilliant and wanted him to like me. It just didn't work. Jan laughed when I tried to impress him with a few quotations from Buddha, and said I should just sit down and keep my trap shut and see if I thought it was for me. So I kept my trap shut and sat down, but I didn't feel peaceful and relaxed, just nearly round the bend with nothing but idiotic thoughts that I could no longer ignore because everything was suddenly so quiet.

When I told Jan, he laughed even more and asked me

if I fancied meeting his meditation teacher. Of course I
did. Jan's meditation teacher was a very small man from
Thailand with the friendliest face I've ever seen. I didn't
understand a word he said, but when I sat down next to
him, I felt really peaceful inside, not just around me. Perhaps I could have found peace in a bathtub, if it hadn't
been for those heating elements. Meditation means more
or less 'heading for the middle', but Jan says the Tibetan
word means getting used to something. I liked that better
than 'bus stop' or 'supermarket till', and since then I've
tried to make meditation a habit. I light a candle and set
down little stones for the people I want to have with me.
I have a Dad stone and a Mum stone, one for guests,
and recently also a very small one for Paul – but if it has
to be, my stones can also stand in for different people.
Because I was worried that the stones idea might be
unBuddhist I asked Jan about it, but he told me there
was actually nothing you could do wrong in Buddhism as
long as you kept more or less to the five *S las*, the exercises
for correct behaviour: not to kill or injure a living crea-
ture; not to take anything that wasn't given to you; not to
hurt anyone through your sexual behaviour; not to lie and
to pay attention to your words; and to turn away from
everything that intoxicated or befuddled. But he also
knew a few Buddhists who enjoyed a schnitzel from time
to time, said Jan, when he saw my face, but in fact I'd been
startled by the bit about sexual behaviour. When I got
home I sat down at the computer and Googled the five

*S las* and was quite relieved when I found out that being secretly in love with Jan was fine as long as I didn't sexually molest him.

I sat down cross-legged on the floor, after I'd lit a tea light and set down the first of my four stones for Joschi. I shut my eyes, but something still wasn't right, so I opened them again and picked up the next stone for my grandmother Lotte and set it down next to Joschi. My grandparents, I thought, but somehow that wasn't quite it, and I picked up another stone and set it down a little further away: that was my grandpa Karl. Then I had to think about Louise and Hannah's mother Frieda, but now I was slowly running out of stones. I still had one, and Louise got it. A weird non-flowering plant stood on the floor next to the window, its pot filled with reddish-brown clay balls: perfect for Frieda. And another one for Hannah, one for Gabor, one for my mother and one for me, while we were about it. Of course my father and Paul, whose personal stones I had allocated out, were still missing, so that meant two more balls. My family. In my mind I apologized to my father's parents for not giving them a space on my altar, but I don't think they even wanted one. I closed my eyes. I opened them again and rearranged the stones: Joschi in the middle and around him Lotte, Frieda and Louise. Now it struck me that I'd forgotten Tamás and Véra and their mother, today of all days, so I got up again, fetched three little balls and set one down for Joschi's wives and the two others behind them, just as

Joschi's other children settled behind their mothers. As I settled behind mine, with Paul and my father and Karl next to me.

The stones were set out in such a way that they looked like a cross, with a strange bubble blowing out at one end. I didn't like that at all, so I closed my eyes and took a deep breath. Exactly two breaths later my mother opened the door to the room.

'Good morning,' she whispered. 'Shall I go away again?'

'No, please stay, it's not working anyway,' I said quickly. My mother was holding two cardboard cups of milky coffee, the sight of which made me feel really cheerful. She threw her jacket on the bed, bent down to me and kissed me. Then she took a look at my altar.

'You've been busy this morning.'

I told her who the individual stones were.

'There's someone missing,' my mother said. 'May I?' She took another clay ball from the flowerpot and set it down beside Joschi's wives. Now there were five of them.

'Joschi's first wife was Tamás's mother,' she said. 'Her name was Mátild and she died quite young. Then, when Joschi married Margit, Tamás was already five, and a short time later Véra was born. That was in 1940, and you know the rest.'

'Hang on a minute,' I said. 'So Joschi was married to Tamás's mother first. Was she Jewish too?'

'As far as I know, yes.'

'And then Joschi married Margit and they had Véra, and a few years later Margit was deported to Auschwitz with the two children, and killed there. Right?'

'Right.'

'Then each of Joschi's children had a different mother,' I said, and straightened up to five stones. Behind each of the five lay another one. I took Karl, Paul and my father back out again, because they no longer fitted the picture. Instead I put their stones in my trouser pocket to have them really close to me. That strange cross had disappeared.

'Now it's a five-branched star,' I said. 'With one longer than the others.'

'That's you,' said my mother and got back to her feet. 'That's the spot where Joschi's star goes on growing.'

'But if I have more than one child I'm going to ruin the whole pattern,' I said.

'Then just give your second child to Hannah,' my mother suggested. 'There's still room behind her.'

While I was showering, I tried to imagine how that strange arrangement between Joschi, Louise and Alfred had come about. Transferring your own child to a different husband, to whom you also had to return your wife, it sounded like a Greek tragedy. On the other hand there only seemed to have been one real loser in this deal, and that was Gabor. Perhaps Joschi had never loved Gabor, and he was fine about being able to surrender him to Alfred. Perhaps Joschi didn't want to have any more children for the time being, and Gabor had just had the bad luck to come into the world too early, when the other children had been dead for three years. Nevertheless, Joschi's lack of interest in Gabor didn't fit with the image I had of my grandfather, not with the generosity and affection that my mother sometimes talked about. And not at all with the grim resolution with which he liked to come to her rescue. At the time, in fact, my mother had felt that it was an inappropriate interference in her private life, but when I imagine Joschi coming into a pub with a furious expression on his face and escorting my underage mother from the premises in front of the eyes of her puzzled friends, it's pretty impressive. Someone who didn't care about his children wouldn't do that.

My mother was lying on the bed when I came out of the bathroom.

'Mum?' I asked. 'Do you think Joschi really didn't want to have any more children after the others had been killed?'

My mother jack-knifed bolt upright. 'That's exactly what I was wondering,' she said. 'And I think, no, he didn't want to have any more children. And then he kept starting things with young women who desperately wanted children. What madness.'

'You mean he didn't even want you?' I asked and sat down next to her on the bed.

'No, not even me. Lotte was the one who was so keen on it, particularly since she'd had a miscarriage the year before,' said my mother. 'But if I'm being honest, I'd have to say that I don't remember a single moment when Joschi gave me the feeling of being unwelcome.'

'But you argued a lot,' I objected.

'And how,' she said. 'But that didn't start until much later, when I was fourteen or fifteen. When I hear Hannah and Gabor's stories, I think I was incredibly lucky. I had him – or at least what was left of him. They didn't have him.'

I remembered my dream, and told it to her. At first she laughed, and then she hugged me. 'Little Lily,' she said. 'This is going to be quite a weird weekend, and I'm pretty sure there's more to come. Are you sure you want to stay? Trains to Berlin leave every two hours, I think.'

'Are you insane?' I asked furiously. 'I'm the only one here with an official job to do, and you want to send me home?'

'Oh, yeah, your presentation,' said my mother. 'I'd completely forgotten about that, with all the family stories. What time is it, actually? We've arranged to meet for breakfast downstairs at half-past nine.'

She rolled sideways off the bed and disappeared into the bathroom.

'You've got exactly five minutes!' I called after her. She said something I didn't catch. It was probably: 'I'm sure I'll just need four.'

Oh yes, my Buchenwald presentation. I'd nearly forgotten it myself, even though it was a piece of homework I'd volunteered to do, partly for less than noble reasons. I admit, I sometimes enjoy being able to say my grandfather was Jewish and in a concentration camp. If you have a Jewish grandfather you're automatically one of the good guys, at least in my school. I'm not so stupid as to admit something like that to a gang of skinheads, but in everyday life it does have its advantages. People are caught off-guard, they're sometimes sympathetic or even respectful, and if the situation is right my arguments also become more effective. Who's going to contradict the granddaughter of a victim of the Nazis, when she warns of the dangers of the far right in her Ethics class? No one who doesn't want to risk serious bother with the school authorities. My mother once said that during her time at university she was let off the hook because she was always on the right side, while some of her fellow students turned away in shame and infernal torment because their parents had been Nazis or fellow travellers. That's exactly what I mean. I'm a third-generation victim, so I thought it was a good idea to raise my average marks with a passionate article about Buchenwald concentration camp, seeing as I was there anyway. In my rucksack I had a brand new notebook in which unfortunately the only things written so far were the stupid notes 'What career?' and 'Archive!', but that would all change after breakfast.

It only took my mother twenty-one minutes – her personal best, at least in my presence. I was very strict and refused to let her dry her hair, and we set off just twenty minutes late for the breakfast room. We took the stairs, and when we reached the ground floor she held me tight and said, 'If I could wish for something today, it would be serenity.'

My mother is a Buddhist as well, in spite of the intoxicating substances that she sometimes succumbs to. She just doesn't know it. There are lots of people like that, Jan says.

# 7

SINCE WE'D BEEN IN HANNAH'S CAR, Gabor hadn't stopped rubbing his fingers: first with the thumb and forefinger of his right hand, each individual finger on his left, then switching around, a short pause and then all over again from the beginning. I was sitting on the back seat beside him, and it was only by summoning up all my willpower that I managed, after endless minutes, to take my eye off his monotonous movements. Gabor looked out of the side window. The rubber band that held his pony-tail in place was so tight that his hair lay completely flat against his scalp. It must have really hurt. He was wearing a blue windcheater over his brown jacket, and was the only one to have brought an umbrella, which was wedged upright between his knees. He was probably going to need it too. The sky was grey; the clouds were low. Behind us lay Weimar and a breakfast we had eaten together, monosyllabically. Ahead of us were the Ettersberg and Buchenwald.

After a few kilometres the road branched off to the left. A sign told us that we were now on 'Blood Road', but I didn't feel like pointing it out to the others and uttering that ugly name. Instead I wrote it down in my notebook. On both sides of the road was forest, nothing but German forest. I couldn't see any of the beech trees that had given it its name. I wound the window down: it smelt of damp soil and mushrooms and rotting leaves. I like that smell. It doesn't make me think of farewells or death, and not even of autumn, just of forest. A forest never smells more like itself than it does in October, and this was no exception.

The higher we climbed, the foggier it became. There was a Dutch coach in front of us. On the left a sign appeared to the monument with the bell-tower, but the bus didn't turn off, it just drove on, so presumably we were heading for the same destination. I couldn't hold my tongue any longer. And besides, I had an assignment.

'Can anyone tell me when exactly Joschi came to Buchenwald?'

The answer from in front came in sync and in two voices: 'Autumn '43'.

'Oh, thanks,' I said and wrote down *Autumn '43*.

'Listen, just how naïve are you lot?' asked Gabor, and it was so unexpected that everyone gave a start and Hannah even braked for a moment. 'The Germans didn't occupy Hungary until the spring of 1944. Doesn't that strike you as a bit strange?'

A gaping abyss had suddenly opened up between the front and back halves of Hannah's car. I had, because of our seating arrangement, inadvertently ended up on Gabor's continental shelf.

'And what do you mean by that?' Hannah asked, and considered Gabor in the rear-view mirror with a face that suggested he'd just been bellowing Nazi slogans.

Before Gabor could reply, my mother said, 'Come on, you must admit there are a few inconsistencies in this respect.'

'Which ones?' Hannah asked severely.

'Well, there's the business about the German occupation of Hungary. Up until that point, of course, the Hungarians hadn't treated their Jewish population particularly kindly, but the deportations didn't start until mid-'44, under German rule. And then there's all the different information that Joschi gave the authorities about the time between 1940 and 1945.'

'So what?' said Hannah. 'Are we about to start calculating how long a Jew actually had to spend in a concentration camp or a labour camp to be considered a respectable victim? For most people a night would be enough to be

75

traumatized for life. And that includes the journey there in a cattle truck.'

'Of course,' said my mother. 'But we still can't say with any certainty what's true in Joschi's claims and what isn't.'

Gabor said nothing more. I wondered what scenes might have been played out in the bar during my absence, given that the mood this morning was so dreadful. Then I wrote *Length of stay unclear*, and then again *Archive* in my notebook, this time with three exclamation marks.

'Could we just leave it as it is for the time being?' asked Hannah, and turned right into the camp car park. 'I suggest you take a look at this place, and if you need any further clarification let's talk about it.'

We had arrived after driving for less than twenty minutes. I could hardly believe that this terrible place and the harmless little town down in the valley were so close to one another. What had the citizens of Weimar imagined was going on up there on their local mountain? How much contempt or stupidity or fear did you need not even to want to know something like that?

My mother also seemed to think it had all gone too quickly. 'Hang on a minute,' she protested. 'I don't think I want to go in there yet.'

'You'll manage,' said Hannah, and turned off the engine.

'I'm not sure about that,' said my mother.

'Sorry, but couldn't you have sorted all this out before?' Gabor asked irritably.

'I want to go in,' I said and opened the car door.

It had started to drizzle slightly. The Dutch coach, which had parked not far away from us, was spewing out its passengers, one after the other. Hardly any of them looked less than seventy, and many of them had some kind of walking aid. Each of them, as they got out, first glanced suspiciously at the big buildings that fanned out facing the car park, holding up the people behind them. The buildings were painted a bright yellow, struggling in vain to create a cheerful impression. Perhaps the effect worked better in the summer, when the weather was nice. The four biggest, three-storey ones, looked almost identical and reminded me of school buildings.

'Those are former SS barracks,' said Hannah. All four of us were standing by the car. Gabor was smoking and studying the barracks through narrowed eyes. My mother took my hand and pressed it for a moment.

'It's all OK,' she said quietly, and attempted a smile that looked too crooked to convince me really.

The visitors' information centre was in one of the two low yellow buildings. As I stepped inside I felt slightly ill, as if the first horror awaited me inside, but it looked like all the other museums I knew. There were brochures in various languages, headsets and audio guides and answers to questions in case you had any. No, unfortunately the archive was closed that weekend, I discovered, but I could always write or phone the archivist's colleagues. I must have looked very disappointed, because the lady at reception changed her tone from professionally friendly to comforting when she handed me a card with the archive phone number and recommended that we visit the exhibition in the former property room – and a map of the camp, because without one it was hard to find your way around the grounds.

'You can phone them first thing on Monday,' my mother said. Of course I could, but I was still frustrated. I was too keen to impress Gabor with a document that said Jószef Molnár really had been imprisoned in Buchenwald in autumn 1943.

'First I'll take you to the tower, and then we'll decide what to do next,' said Hannah, and we walked outside, where the procession of Dutch pensioners had now reached the entrance to the visitors' information centre, completely surrounding Gabor, who had stayed in the car park to smoke. He had to push his way carefully through wheeled Zimmers and walking sticks to reach us, which wasn't easy because the old people seemed to be in a state of shock of some kind: they weren't talking, they weren't moving, they just stood there waiting for someone to come and collect them.

'Shall we go?' asked Hannah. Gabor put up his umbrella and nodded.

We followed Hannah along a narrow path that ran behind the barracks buildings. Most of the trees and bushes still had their yellow autumn foliage. It was so quiet that I could hear the water dripping from the leaves onto the ground. From the corners of my eyes I could make out a few smaller buildings on the left and the right, but because Hannah didn't look as if she was about to say anything I assumed that they weren't important. We turned left, and the path became a paved road, the road expanded into a driveway and all of a sudden there it was, in the wet autumn landscape: the camp gate.

It was all somehow happening too quickly and unexpectedly, I thought, and I was surprised by the sense of outrage that swelled up in me at the sight of it. After all, it was nothing but an ugly utilitarian building with two widespread thighs, each about twenty-five metres long, and a watchtower in the middle above the passageway, with a wooden railing running around it, and above it a little tower with a clock. Four Lego bricks would have been enough to make a copy of the thing, two long white ones and two smaller, shit-brown ones. The windows in the right wing looked like office windows; on the left they were more like peepholes and built quite far at the top and closed off with wooden panels; you could have imagined stables behind them, or something worse, much worse.

None of us said anything, and I was afraid of destroying the silence with my fury. Of course I knew the gate from pictures, everyone in my family knew it; I knew the clock showed a quarter past three because the American troops had turned up to liberate at a quarter past three, and above all I knew what I would see on the cast-iron gate, towards which we were now heading. I tried to imagine I was a prisoner in Buchenwald, coming back to the camp from working in the quarry, but that wasn't a good idea, because it only intensified my fury. So I imagined I was a Buddhist nun, and that actually helped a bit. Suddenly I could breathe again, but with the breaths, regrettably, came the tears, and I didn't want that; I didn't want to go blubbing around the place while we were still at the front gate.

A hand rested on the back of my neck, just for a brief moment, then quickly withdrew again, but that small touch did me good, even if the hand hadn't belonged to the person I expected.

'*Jedem das Seine*: To each his own,' said Gabor. 'I always thought the Nazis had "*Arbeit macht frei*" above the gates of their concentration camps.'

'Buchenwald was the only exception,' Hannah replied. 'For the edification of the inmates, the inscription was set up so that you could read it from inside.'

The gate with the inscription was half closed. It occurred to me that the 'I', 'A' and 'M' were also the only letters you could read from this side. *I am*. I was quite pleased with my discovery.

'It's also a classical principle from Roman law,' said Hannah. 'Just by way of background information.'

'Heavens, you've really done your homework,' said Gabor.

'Yes, and I'm also compulsive and neurotic like all children of former inmates,' said Hannah and took me by the hand, and together we walked through the gate like Alice through the looking glass.

What had I been expecting? Anything, just not that endless expanse behind it, that 'No Longer', where there must once have been so much. An asphalted square with lots of ripped-up surface right in front of us; behind it a desert of stones – no, a cemetery of stones, with huge rectangular pits of rubble that probably corresponded to the outlines of the former barracks, surrounded by more stones and with gravel paths running in between them. Nothing green anywhere, only far away at the end of the grounds the edge of a forest, blurred by the drizzle. The few people walking around, apart from ourselves, crossed the square singly or in groups, shoulders hunched and heads lowered, or walked forlornly around among the rubble pits.

'This was the parade ground,' Hannah said quietly. 'Here the prisoners had to line up in blocks and stand to attention. White stones were set into the ground as markers, they're still there.'

'Please don't give me any directions right now,' said Gabor.

'No problem,' Hannah replied. My mother had shoved her hands deep into her jacket pockets and was staring at the pitted tarmac in front of her feet.

'Would you like a little guided tour through the camp, Lily?' Hannah asked.

'I think I'd really rather walk around on my own for a bit,' I said.

'Me too,' said Gabor. 'See you later.'

We watched after him as he turned left and moved away, his eyes fixed on the ground, gripping the handle of his umbrella with both hands. After a few metres, he had to bend down to tie his shoe, and the way he clumsily set down his umbrella, which was promptly caught by a gust of wind and spun off a good way to the side, really touched me, I couldn't say why.

'What about you?' Hannah asked, looking at my mother.

'Just don't leave me alone right now,' said my mother. 'And by the way I'm very receptive to directions.'

'Come on, then,' said Hannah.

We agreed to meet up later at the exhibition in the big storage depot, and then off the two of them marched, arms linked and quietly talking to one another, and Hannah's bright red silk scarf and her hair were the only patches of colour for far and wide.

It had stopped raining. I opened the brochure with the map and the recommended routes, folded it up again straight away and put it back in my rucksack. I didn't want a description of the path. I didn't even want to know what was what. I just wanted to walk and see and absorb. And I wanted music. I didn't know if it was inappropriate or even disrespectful to go walking around in the grounds and listen to music, but no one would notice anyway. My father had put music on my iPod specially. It was by Arvo Pärt. I didn't know who or what Arvo Pärt was, but my father knew all about music. It was exactly right for such an occasion, he had said.

I was about to set off when the Dutch party reached the gate building behind me. They passed through the entrance two by two, like schoolchildren, led by a guide calling encouraging words to them in Dutch, at least that's what it sounded like. There was a couple holding hands. I counted twenty-nine people. The last one through the gate was a very small, very old woman with a friendly tortoise-face, clinging to her blue-wheeled Zimmer. It took her ages to get to the other side, and when she was there she stopped and struggled to turn her Zimmer so that she could read the inscription. When she turned back around, our eyes met. She nodded to me. She was crying.

I put my headphones on. The first notes hit me right in the middle of the heart.

# 8

I STOOD THERE for quite a long time, unable to make my mind up what direction to take. Behind me to my right was a barbed-wire fence that started at the eastern wing of the gate building and ran more or less in a straight line towards another watchtower. There it took a bend and disappeared behind a wall of bushes and grey drizzle. Right in front of it stood a house with a few low annexes that half vanished into a dip in the ground. It could have been a block of flats with its little windows, a cosy light gleaming behind them, had it not been for that huge chimney that loomed above the roof, visible from a long way off. My stomach clenched and my feet said no and refused to head in that direction, even before my brain managed to tell me what kind of building it must be. In my mind I put crematoria quite high up on the list of places I really didn't want to be, just ahead of space capsules and MRI scanners, and meanwhile I watched the Dutch tour group heading at a snail's pace towards a different building further to the north of the camp grounds.

Back where the forest began there stood a grey block, several storeys high, which looked as if a whole city had once stood around it, and the city had been blown up, leaving only the block. A ghost house whose uniform rows of windows made it look like calculating paper, with dormers like eyes on stalks, staring straight ahead. I knew it was the depot where we had arranged to meet later, and I put depots somewhere in among MRI scanners and solariums and even now I started coming up with reasons not to have to go there later.

So either straight on or to the left.

In the end I chose something in between and approached a couple standing beside a metal plate that was set into the ground and surrounded by faded bouquets. The man was crouched down on the ground. He had a salt-and-pepper beard and was wearing a brightly coloured woollen cap. Real class of '68, I would say. Wasn't Gabor one of those? The women bent over the man and kept trying to brush her damp, curly hennaed hair out of her face, without success. The man solemnly rested one hand on the metal plate, while reading from a brochure at the same time. I turned the music off and took out one earphone because I wanted to hear what he said.

Man: 'Hey, this is incredible. It gives all the countries the prisoners came from, and that thing in the middle is always at 37 degrees. Body temperature, you see?'

Woman: 'Amazing. If it was winter now and there was snow, it'd look amazing. I mean, there'd be no snow on it, would there?'

I decided not to take my earphones out again and crossed the parade ground.

In front of me there stretched miserable barrack-grounds, a succession of featureless, dark fields. I chose the path that ran between the two outside rows to the forest's edge, but I could have taken any other, none of them looked prettier or more inviting than any other. The foundations were edged with narrow stones and carefully filled with black cinders, there was light-coloured gravel, and the squares in front of the buildings, with the numbers of the blocks written on the stone, were covered with reddish gravel. I walked past block 1, block 7 and block 13. It looked very neat and tidy here, but even in its tidiness there still lay the horror of days past. Before, what I'd feared most was the idea that they might have turned it into a kind of Disneyland with wooden barracks you could go into and big puppets in striped prison uniforms playing the part of camp inmates. On my left, far away beneath the trees, I could make out another of those buildings that looked as if it was the only one left standing, but I wasn't going to go into that barrack any more than I was going to go into any of the others.

From a field of gravel on my right, roughly carved stone pillars grew like stalagmites. Most of them wore caps of little pebbles which visitors had put on them. I could read engraved names on the pillars: Treblinka, Gross-Rosen, Neuengamme. Men's and women's voices sang alternately between my left ear and my right. Had there been women in Buchenwald as well? I dimly remembered a remark of Hannah's about a camp brothel, but I didn't know anything about women prisoners.

Block 19, block 25, block 30. I couldn't work out the system by which the blocks were numbered. A glance at the map of the camp would probably have clarified matters, but I didn't care enough to look. After block 30, grass and bushes mingled amongst the stones, and block 36 behind it consisted only of a few decayed remains of its foundation walls. Straight in front of me there was forest. I turned to the right and walked the length of the next block. According to my careful estimates it could easily have been block 37, but in the end I forgot to check because I'd spotted Gabor at the edge of the forest, studying one of the information panels. I didn't have the slightest desire for a meeting, and I was sure he didn't either, so I turned to the right again and made a mental note of the spot so that I might be able to come back and see what it was that had captured Gabor's attention.

88

Now the gate building was within sight, and I could see the class-of-'68 couple again as well, walking around less than twenty metres away from me, both with their eyes fixed on the ground. The woman started gesticulating and called out something to the man which, together with Arvo Pärt's plaintive choirs, sounded very urgent, but he didn't react, instead adopting his favourite posture and squatting down on the ground. After trying in vain once more to attract his interest, the woman walked past him to the end of the block, turned round and came back to him with her head lowered, as if she had lost something important on the way. This time there was a great temptation to look at the map and see what had so fascinated the two of them, but I resisted it. It took half an eternity before they finally withdrew and left the square free for me.

When I reached the front of the block they had just left, I noticed that the area at its base was covered not with dark gravel, but with big, pale shards of stone. The long, north-facing side was bounded by a narrow concrete wall which ran along the path, almost level with the ground. On the inside, a dip in the gravel surface added to its height. It looked as if there was a drain in the middle of the wall, at a depth of about two metres, that was sucking the stone fragments into the earth.

I ignored the information panel that wanted to explain this block to me, and turned towards the side of the building that the man had just been squatting next to. An outsized inscription ran parallel to the little wall along the whole length of the ground plan: words of stone sank into the gravel path. 'Children', it said at my feet. Because I was at the wrong end, I could only read the word backwards as I walked along it. When I had reached the start of the sentence I had to go back a little way until I had really understood it. *'Auf daß erkenne das künftige Geschlecht, die Kinder, die geboren werden, daß sie aufstehen und erzählen ihren Kindern.'* The sentence was twenty-eight paces long and described pretty exactly how things were in our family: Joschi hadn't spoken a single word about it to his children, but my mother and Hannah, the coming generation, had risen up and told their children, namely me.

I still wasn't halfway along the line. The German inscription ran into one in Hebrew, and because I knew that you read Hebrew from right to left, I walked along it in the right direction and pretended to be able to read it. The stone letters looked proud and severe. Hebrew writing looks as if it's been designed by an artist, and some irritable calligrapher has gone over it again afterwards and reduced it to the barest minimum. Because the vowels are left out, everything had been said in eleven paces, and I reached the English sentence, which actually formed the beginning of the row – familiar letters which, in spite of the biblical language, and more than thirty paces, yielded their meaning much faster to me than their German version did: 'So that the generation to come might know, the children, yet to be born, that they too may rise and declare to their children.'

More or less level with the Hebrew text, the wall was covered with pebbles of all sizes and colours. Hannah had told me that there were different theories about the origin of the practice of laying stones for the dead. As far as she knew, the Jewish people in search of the Promised Land had no other choice but to bury their dead in the desert. The piles of stone were conceived as a warning for the priests who were only able to approach a corpse up to a certain distance. Only over time had this become a ritual that said: may my memory of the dead be as constant as the little stone that I have brought for him.

I remembered the three stones I had been carrying in my trouser pocket since that morning. I looked for a fourth and set the stones down on the wall: one for Joschi, one for his wife Margit, one for Véra and one for Tamás. I took a step back. If I unfocused my eyes slightly I could see stars everywhere, nothing but stars made of stones growing into each other.

And now, the depot. There was no point putting off the meeting any longer. In less than ten minutes my mother and Hannah would be there to meet me there on the first floor, and I could be sure that my mother at least would be punctual. I took the brochure out of my rucksack and read: 'In this building newly arrived inmates left everything that they had brought with them, and received uniforms, number and triangular fabric badges. Since its restoration in the mid 1980s the building has served as an exhibition space for the history of the concentration camp.' So anyone planning to write an essay about Buchenwald had better take a look inside. Not least, incidentally, someone who had an appointment there.

A low rectangle, perhaps five metres by five, granted me a brief pause. A stone block inside bore the inscription 'Goethe's Oak', probably meaning the stout tree stump in the middle of the square. It was news to me that the Nazis liked Goethe. Had the whole camp been built around this fine old German oak? Had they hanged people from it or let their Alsatians pee against it? At that moment the clouds parted, and the tree stump shone in the midday sun. With its cement filling it looked like an old, worn tooth. I was sure it must often have wished they would dig it up at last – root and branch – instead of displaying it here as Goethe's Oak.

Arvo Pärt's choirs had fallen silent. When I turned round to face the depot, to my great relief I saw my mother coming towards me, alone. She was waving at me.

I hadn't thought about Jan once.

They always said my mother was convinced, even as a child, that the survival of her family depended on her being the only one who was able to keep her head. I couldn't remember ever seeing her crying in public, let alone in her sleep. Even in the cinema she managed to let her tears flow as discreetly and casually as if they actually belonged to someone else whom she had very kindly allowed to borrow her cheeks. Then, when I spoke to her and she turned her face towards me, she was already smiling again. She was smiling now too. She had tired, red eyes.

'Just imagine, Lily,' she said, 'they've got this kind of glass case, like an endlessly long table with a glass plate on top of it, and it contains the objects from the camp that they dug up afterwards. Buttons. Mostly buttons. As if people were creatures who were always losing buttons, even in a place like this.'

I imagined men in striped prison uniforms, with buttons flying off their jackets. I saw them creeping around on the floor looking for their buttons.

'Every now and again a few coins. Home-made combs. A little agate heart. And then these false teeth.'

Now it was teeth that the striped men were looking for, their jackets open, toothless.

'Sort of metal false teeth that you could stick in your lower jaw, I think. Three or four artificial teeth on each side and a clamp at the front. God, I don't know why that got to me so much. More than anything else on show up there. And that's saying quite a lot.'

'You told me Joschi lost all his teeth back then,' I said.

'Yes, maybe that's it.' She threw her head back and looked up at the grey walls. 'There are lots of photographs from the camp up there. I scanned them all from top to bottom to see if Joschi's face was among them. I know I'd spot him if he was in one of the pictures. And at the same time I was so scared he would be.'

'But he was nowhere to be seen.'

'No, he wasn't. Unfortunately.'

'And where is Hannah?'

'She's been adopted – by a little Dutchwoman with a Zimmer on wheels. They were still talking when I left. Hannah said she'd come to reception afterwards and wait for us there. In half an hour.' She looked at her watch. 'So we've got at least an hour. Have you any idea where Gabor might be?'

'I saw him before,' I said. 'I didn't want to bother him, and that's why I left, but I'd like to go there again. It's over there towards the trees.'

'The Small Camp must be over there too,' said my mother. 'I'll come with you.'

We took a path that ran parallel to the edge of the forest. On our left was the sea of stone with all the barracks, on our right grass-covered hills of rubble and here and there excavations that revealed not temple complexes but only more foundations of ugly buildings with ugly names. Hygiene Institute. Typhus Serum Institute. Meanwhile my mother talked about the exhibition. She found it impressive and shocking. None the less, she shared my opinion that I could spare myself a visit to it.

'You can write about it without having been there,' she said. 'If you like, you can use my story about the buttons and the false teeth.'

We Molnárs are like that: generous in passing on the copyright on our stories.

'What sort of Small Camp is it?' I asked. 'Do you know anything more about it?'

'A bit. That famous photograph of the half-dead camp inmates lying in their rabbit hutches, staring bewilderedly into the liberators' camera, that's from the Small Camp. The barracks in the actual camp were like luxury bungalows compared with the accommodation here. This was where they suffered and died.'

'More than over there?' I asked and pointed at the foundations of the main camp.

'I think it was bad enough over there,' said my mother. 'But here it must have been pure hell. It was a collection camp and a transhipment centre for new arrivals. Most of the people here were Jews. Many of them came from Auschwitz. They knew what would happen to the ones they left behind. From here they were sent on to other concentration camps or labour camps.'

'So was Joschi in the Small Camp as well? You said he was in Buchenwald first of all, and that he spent the last six months of the war as a forced labourer in the Harz Mountains.'

'That's true, but you didn't actually spend a whole year in a transit camp. It was a place to get away from or die in, not a place to stay.'

I remembered Gabor's remark about his journey there. So did my mother, I could see that.

'How do you know when Joschi was in Buchenwald, if he never talked to you about it?'

'From his effects. There's a carbon copy of the authori-
zation of his compensation claim. That was in the early
1950s. In it he gave a solemn declaration of when he'd
been imprisoned in which camp and for how long. His
account is rather vague, but it's lengthy enough. It starts in
1941.'

'And why did you never try and find out whether there
were any other documents about him?'

My mother stopped by an information panel. 'Look,
there's something here about the Small Camp. The
memorial must be back there.'

First I wanted an answer. 'Why did you never ask?'

'Because I gave up asking as a child.' She smiled, but
her frown deepened noticeably. 'Or perhaps because I
didn't want to reveal any of Joschi's dark secrets.'

'What kind of dark secrets?'

'Lily,' said my mother. 'On one point Gabor is definitely
right: that Joschi's statements about his time in the camp
weren't 100 per cent correct. Whether he wanted to get
more compensation money or cover something else up, I
don't know. But I think I have to respect that in the end,
even if it means that I'll never find out what actually happened back then.'

'Does that mean you think he wasn't even here in
Buchenwald?'

'No, I think he was. Just as I'm sure that his wife and
children were killed in Auschwitz. As Hannah said, that
in itself is enough to finish you off for the rest of your life.'

I asked her about the previous evening in the hotel bar. My mother had a think.

'It could be that it put Gabor in a bad mood. But Hannah didn't get particularly far into her story. I think he took his leave at the point when her mother makes her learn all the concentration camp locations when she's six.'

But a scene like that would have made anyone run off, I thought. Whatever might have prompted Hannah's mother to bring up her daughter so obsessively as a Jewish child – even now I don't understand it. My mother suspects that it meant Frieda was able to persuade herself that she had a special commission to fulfil, and for a Catholic that definitely sounds better than having an illegitimate child. Hannah in turn says it didn't do her any harm finding out about things like that at the age of six, but she had suffered from the fact that she wasn't able to talk to anyone about it. Her Jewish descent had been topic number one and at the same time it had been top secret. I can think of hardly anything that could make you even lonelier.

We walked a little way into the forest that grew behind the Small Camp.

'I know it sounds crazy,' my mother said after a while. 'But now that we're finally here I can make my peace with this place. At least I can make a start. Do you know what I mean?'

I couldn't help thinking of those sentences in stone.

'Come on, let me show you something else,' I said and took her hand. We turned round.

On our right, the class-of-'68 couple appeared on the cobbled path leading to the memorial of the Small Camp. The man walked ahead, the woman a few steps behind him. She said, 'OK, I've been walking around long enough in the camp, Wolfgang. Let's go inside some-where. We haven't seen the crematorium yet. I'm sure it'll be warmer in there than it is out here.'

Wolfgang's answer got stuck somewhere in his beard. We looked at each other. Reflected in my mother's face I saw my own bewilderment, and then she suddenly exploded, and she laughed and laughed until the tears ran down her face. She didn't bother wiping them away. There was no doubt they were her own.

# 9

TWO THINGS STRUCK ME after we had left the car park behind us and were driving back along the Blood Road towards Weimar. The first thing was that after *Archive!!!* I hadn't written another single word in my notebook. So I would have to rely on my memory and the stack of brochures from visitor information. That was plainly doable, but also a bit shaming, particularly since my attempts to take photographs of the inscription over the camp gate had yielded nothing useful, because people had been constantly going in and out. My mother, who has highly sensitive antennae for such matters, turned to me and asked, 'Have you actually collected enough material for your essay?' Then I remembered the second thing: my mother looked contented, or more precisely she looked like someone who had just slain a really fat dragon. One of the kind that's been lying around in the road with its breath stinking. Or perhaps the one who had always guarded the gate into Buchenwald.

'I completely forgot to take any notes.' If she was killing dragons already, at least I would have to confess to my incompetence. 'But I'll get something together anyway.'

'Of course you will,' said Hannah, looking for my face in the rear-view mirror. 'Your own experience counts. Just start with your grandfather's story.'

'Aaargh,' said Gabor. He sounded infinitely annoyed. It hadn't been hard to find him in the camp grounds; he had been standing by the car park, smoking, as if he had never left the spot. I'd have bet on it, if I hadn't known otherwise. In the half hour that we still had to wait for Hannah, Gabor had been absent and withdrawn, and I hadn't even risked talking to him. Instead, I had called my father and out of sheer enthusiasm that my mother had called out, 'Say hello from me', I had left him a rather silly message on his voicemail, which would certainly make him think when he listened to it.

We reached the turn-off for Weimar. At the end – or rather at the beginning – of the Blood Road there stood a reddish stone obelisk that I'd missed on the way there. It seemed to date from the days of the GDR and looked like a dirty finger showing off.

'What would you say to a coffee?' Hannah hadn't missed Gabor's comment, I could tell that from her frown in the rear-view mirror, but clearly she didn't want to get the discussion going all over again, at least not in her car. My mother had never refused anybody a coffee in her life, Hannah knew that, and in that respect I was getting more and more like her.

Hannah knew that too, but even so I said, 'Yeah, that'd be great', just so that someone said something. Gabor's answer came a few hours later, and again it was more of a noise than a clear statement. I heard it as 'OK', and Hannah plainly did too, because at the last minute she turned off not to Weimar but in the opposite direction. Our journey ended ten minutes and three villages later at Annis' Coffee House.

'By the way, Anni is Peggy's sister, in case you didn't know,' Hannah said to me as we got out.

'But she's engaged to Sammy at the hotel bar,' I maintained. 'So be careful.'

Anni was wearing a tracksuit, she owned a gleaming Italian espresso machine and could have been Sammy's grandmother. That reminded me once again of the Dutchwoman with the wheeled Zimmer. I asked Hannah about her.

'Her name was Bella. Her husband had been in Buchenwald. Up until his death he talked about practically nothing else. She knew all the stories from the camp off by heart. He died last year, and she finally wanted to see the place she'd been married to for almost fifty years.'

'So more or less the opposite of our father,' said my mother and cautiously tasted her cappuccino, paused for a moment and then took another sip. 'The coffee is good. I'll forgive her that misplaced apostrophe.'

'Our father didn't tell us any stories from Buchenwald because clearly there was nothing to tell,' Gabor said and started stirring the contents of his cup like mad.

'Aunt Louise always did that too when things got a bit dramatic,' my mother said, startled. 'Hey, Gabor, you're like Louise! Come on then, get it all out.'

Hannah's facial expression reminded me of Michel Friedman, the German-Jewish politician. *If you make one single mistake, boy, I'll get you by the balls.*

Gabor clearly found my mother's comment irrelevant and stopped stirring. 'Alfred told me,' he said, and his voice was shrill and even a little tremulous, 'that the whole business about Joschi's Jewishness was invented. Yes, he had been married to Jewish women and had children with them, and that business about Auschwitz might have happened too, but Joschi himself wasn't a Jew. He and Louise came up with that so that Joschi would at least get a bit of compensation from the German state.'

'How original,' said Hannah. Her voice dripped with sarcasm. 'Did Alfred remember that on his deathbed, and tell you with his last breath so that at least one person would know the truth?'

'No, not on his deathbed.' Gabor's spoon started clatter-
ing against the edge of his cup again. 'Not his, anyway. It
was just after Joschi's death.'

'What exactly did he say?' asked my mother.

'It was about Joschi's funeral. Alfred said the bastard
had managed to get himself buried in a Jewish cemetery on
top of everything else – it was the height of impertinence.'

My mother started giggling quietly. Hannah flashed
her a warning glance.

'When I asked him what he meant, Alfred said Joschi's
Jewish biography was a pack of lies. In reality Joschi had
been a little Hungarian trade unionist who couldn't keep
his big trap shut and who was, to make matters worse,
married to a Jewish woman, which would have brought
him a few months' forced labour. A sad business, yes, but
not enough to get you compensation. So they made Joschi
a Jew. It can't have been all that difficult, all the witnesses
were dead, after all.'

'And what did Louise say about Alfred's revelation?'
my mother wanted to know.

'Louise?' Gabor replied. 'Louise wasn't even there, and
I never talked to her about it afterwards either. She would
have denied everything anyway.'

'Gabor, you don't seriously believe all this crap, do
you?' Hannah was slowly getting annoyed.

'And why not?' Red patches were appearing on Gabor's
face. 'Please prove me the contrary! Is there a birth certificate for Joschi? No. Are there any documents apart

Susann Pásztor

from his own statements? No. There's nothing but a pile of crappy myths that his wives spread about the place. And his daughters, I might add.'

Hannah had reared up like a cobra. Before she could strike, my mother said, 'It made me laugh a moment ago because I couldn't help thinking about the conversation I had with the rabbi on the day of Joschi's funeral. Lotte had always been firmly convinced that Joschi was a half-Jew —'

'Half-Jew is a bloody Nazi word,' Hannah cut in with a hiss.

'OK. So, at any rate, Joschi had always told her his father was a Jew and his mother wasn't. Up until then it had never occurred to me or Lotte that according to this theory Joschi couldn't be a proper Jew. It was right before the funeral, we were sitting in the rabbi's study, and the rabbi wanted to have information about Joschi's life that he could use in his funeral address. So Lotte told him about his wife and his children who had been deported to Auschwitz, and then she told him something about Budapest and Joschi's Jewish father and his mother, but she hadn't been Jewish, she had been a immigrant Swabian farmer's daughter.'

I imagined my grandmother explaining our family background.

'The rabbi turned pale when she said that, and said no, no, he didn't want to hear anything about that now. Lotte was a bit irritated and so was I, and it was only much later that I worked out that she had almost talked him out of his place in the Jewish cemetery.'

'Anyone who can't demonstrate that he had a Jewish mother isn't even accepted by the Jewish community,' said Hannah, who might have been expected to know. 'And that would be the end of the matter, wouldn't it? And even Swabian farmers can have Jewish daughters, if you'll forgive me saying so.'

Gabor hadn't given up, not by a long way. 'My goodness, Hannah, just imagine you've got a Hungarian forced labourer standing in front of you, without a passport, without any family papers, claiming he's a Jew. Why wouldn't they take him in? They were probably glad of anyone who was still alive.'

'So they just had a look in his underpants to see if he'd been circumcised and left it at that? Forget it, Gabor, no rabbi responsible for accepting people into the community is going to be as amateurish as that.'

'And was he even circumcised?' asked Gabor.

'Ah, can I ask something?' I said. 'Do you have any idea when Joschi joined the Jewish community? Perhaps he only did it after he had separated from Lotte – so at some point just before his death, when he had already had years of compensation. After all, the thing Gabor was talking about was just after the war. It could be that in those days the German authorities would have been much more likely to accept that he was a Jew if he said so. They'd also be bound to have a guilty conscience if someone showed up and said he'd been in a camp and he didn't have any papers.'

'Your grandfather *was* a Jew, Lily, there's absolutely no doubt about that,' Hannah said resolutely.

Now Gabor really got into gear. 'You're not in charge of all the definitions, my dear girl,' he said. 'In the end all you know is what your Mummy told you. Just because it fits in more nicely with your biography, you still can't prove what really happened back then.'

'None of us knows more than what Mum told them,' said my mother. 'Apart from you – you still have those Alfred-truths. But you wouldn't get far with him as a neutral witness.'

Gabor knocked back his coffee in one. 'But unlike you the idea of being Jewish doesn't do anything for me. I think it stops you seeing straight.'

'There were actually times when I doubted that Joschi was really a Jew,' my mother said quietly.

'What?' Hannah looked at her, annoyed. 'What are you on about now? In many respects our father may not have, shall we say, fully come up to our expectations, but to call his Jewish identity into question now strikes me as practically indecent.'

'Oh, come on, Hannah,' my mother said. 'We really know so little. The only thing we can say with any certainty is that he was a great twister of truths. He told your mother that as a ten-year-old orphan he was brought up as a Catholic by his elder sister and her Christian husband. He told my mother he was the son of an affluent Jewish businessman and his non-Jewish wife. I've no idea what he told Louise . . .'

'Big Jewish families from the 7th district of Budapest –
poverty-stricken,' says Gabor. 'Eight brothers and sisters.
All died in the Holocaust.'

'But his brother sometimes used to call us,' said my
mother.

'You see!' said Gabor.

Hannah dropped her cup on the table with a crash.
'That's all water under the bridge,' she cried. 'Of course
he lied like a trooper. Each of his wives got a different
biography from him, the one that suited her best. Each of
his wives cobbled together her own story from what he
told them and gave us that. Who could blame him if he
never wanted to talk about that terrible past again?'

'Me,' said my mother. 'I blamed him. Lots, in fact.
Especially after his death. Your father dies, you've just
turned eighteen, and you know nothing about him – nothing, nothing, nothing.'

'And you're the only one of us who spent years living
right at the source, so don't complain,' said Hannah. 'Perhaps it was your interviewing technique.'

'I hadn't got an interviewing technique. I didn't even
ask any questions.'

'And what led you to doubt Joschi's Jewish origins?'
Gabor wouldn't let go.

My mother thought for a moment. 'There was never a
concrete reason,' she said. 'I always started getting doubt-
ful when I realized that I was identifying sentimentally or
self-righteously with my Jewish roots, when I was telling

stories that Joschi had told. Then I always thought, hey, you don't even really know. He lied about so many things, why not about this too?'

'Because you don't just think up things like that,' said Hannah. 'Because it would have been so incredibly cynical to jump on that bandwagon after such a tragedy, just to get yourself a few financial advantages. I don't think he was capable of that, do you?'

Gabor said nothing. My mother said, 'No. I think it's OK to speculate about it, but I don't really think he was capable of it.'

'Yeah, that's really reassuring,' replied Hannah. She ignored Gabor's silence.

'Even so, what I don't understand today,' said my mother, 'is the odd pattern of his repression. Nothing about Joschi really fits with what I know about traumatized Nazi victims. Some never let go of the subject, like Bella's husband from Buchenwald. I knew one whose father was an artist and survived Auschwitz. Afterwards he just painted Auschwitz paintings, one after the other. In my naïvety I told the son I envied him for the open way the subject was discussed in his family. He was horrified and asked me if I'd lost my marbles.' My mother gave Anni a sign that was supposed to mean she felt it was time for another cappuccino. 'But most survivors preferred not to say anything. And for some reason Joschi preferred to use outrageous stories to – what? Embellish his past? Conceal it? I assume Louise was the one most familiar with his real biography.

Afterwards Hannah's mother was presented with the little-orphan version, and my mother got only the half Jew. After that he plainly stopped talking about it altogether. With his children he didn't even start.'

'Perhaps he wanted to protect you,' I said.

'It's funny, Lotte once said something similar to me,' my mother replied. 'That was after Hannah showed up and this whole business got under way. I wanted her to tell me why no one had mentioned that Joschi was a Jew and that he'd been in a camp. My mother said she'd wanted to protect me. According to the motto, the less the child knows the better. Even then I thought it was completely nuts.'

'Why?' I asked.

'Because ignorance never protects you. Joschi must have known that better than anyone. And if ignorance was the goal, then why have we had photographs of Véra and Tamás on our walls at home for as long as I can remember?'

'What? He put them up at your house too?' Hannah asked in disbelief. 'I always thought you'd found them in some cupboard somewhere and didn't know who they were.'

'They were there from the start, little Véra and little Tamás,' said my mother. 'So poor, so dead. And I tell you, I couldn't stand the two of them.'

# 10

OF COURSE I KNEW THE pictures of Véra and Tamás.
They were photographs taken in the early 1940s in a
Budapest photographic studio: hand-coloured, says my
mother. Two prints hang in Hannah's flat, along with the
famous Joschi-casts-his-shadow photo and lots of other
family pictures beside the dining table. You can only find
them at our house after looking for a long time, and then
only when you work out my mother's complicated storage
system. Pictures have to travel, she says. So the pictures in
our flat are constantly on the move, they wander from
walls into drawers and onto shelves and from there back
to another wall. My mother illustrates books, and her

drawings first have to go on a long journey before they can appear in a book. She says she's never lost a picture in her life so far. There's also a big box for weary pictures that have already been around a bit. That was where I last saw Véra and Tamás.

I've always been particularly fond of that picture of Véra, but my mother says she used to find Véra completely idiotic with her old-fashioned red velvet dress and that huge bow that looked like a propeller-blade on her blonde curly hair. She said she even preferred grinning Tamás with his sticking-out ears. But apart from their names she had no idea who these children even were. The pictures hung as naturally on her parents' bedroom wall as the stars in the sky, and after all you didn't ask how the stars got there unless you were a bit stupid, and even though at some point she discovered that Véra and Tamás were children of Joschi's, and that they'd been dead for a very, very long time, she didn't ask any more questions, but with people who had been dead for a very long time you really didn't admit that you'd always been furiously jealous of them without knowing why. Hannah once told me that while my mother might have been a noisy, obstreperous rebel when they met at fourteen, she was also surrounded by an incredible cluelessness about her own family history.

'When as a child I asked Joschi anything about himself, it was always followed by a stubborn silence, or a long, abstruse string of fairytale lies,' my mother had said after

I told her about Hannah's remark. 'I just started making sense of things for myself.'

Making sense of things meant, amongst other things, that my mother sometimes answered questions in the class yearbook about her father's job by saying that he was a private detective – sometimes that he was an inventor, bookmaker or pensioner – even though for a long time she had assumed that he was a bank robber on the run because he would never tell her how he had lost the little finger on his left hand. Joschi for his part went on embellishing the legend, by presenting himself at parents' evenings as an experienced educator or a passionate scientist. In fact, since my mother's birth, he had been a house husband and full-time father, and my grandmother Lotte supported the family with her teaching income. My mother had the most modern parents in the whole village, but that didn't count for much in the school yearbooks of the 1960s.

Hannah had a similar problem, incidentally, but in her case it was a complete father that she entered in her year-book for the first time in year seven, in the column that had been empty for years. Because the first time they met he had claimed that he dealt in jewellery and gemstones, described himself as a jeweller and even held her teacher's sceptical glance. The following year, for safety's sake, she switched to 'businessman' and stuck with that for the rest of her schooldays.

So, Hannah's story. It was very important to me that Gabor knew more, even if it meant that I would now have to take my Buddhist *S las* to the max and make myself look entirely clueless.

'I bet you talked about it last night, the way Holmes found out the truth about Watson, didn't you?'

My mother darted me an amused glance.

'We did what?' asked Gabor.

'We didn't even get to my first day at school,' said Hannah.

'Excuse me, who are Holmes and Watson?' Gabor looked as if he was expecting the worst, possibly more children of Joschi's.

'That would be Mum and Hannah,' I replied. 'Do you know how they met?'

'At some point yesterday there was talk about people snuffling around in living-room cupboards,' said Gabor. 'Ah, now I understand. Holmes and Watson.'

'Hannah started first. When she was about eleven, she found bank statements showing maintenance payments, though her mother had always told her that her father had died in a car accident before he could marry her. Her mother freaked out a bit when that came out, but Hannah still managed to engineer a meeting with Joschi. That's what happened, right?'

'Entirely correct,' Hannah confirmed. 'And once the story was out in the open, Frieda filled in the rest and told me about my father's true nature, that he was a conman, a liar, a traitor, a gambler, a good-for-nothing. Someone who failed to reveal that he was married to someone else and got not just his wife, but his lover too, pregnant almost at the same time.'

'And she wasn't even wrong there,' said Gabor. 'But she agreed that he was Jewish?'

'That was the only thing she never questioned. I could spell Bergen-Belsen before I learned to tie my shoelaces. Instead of children's picture books, my mother insisted on giving me books of photographs about the Holocaust. For eleven years I was the daughter of a dead Jewish hero, and now all of a sudden I was the daughter of a living Jewish ladies' man.'

And just as lonely as you were before, I thought.

'And what was your first meeting with him like?'

Wonderful – it was all quite natural. Gabor asked questions, Hannah answered.

'Very strange. I was shocked at how old he was already. He was so different from the way I'd imagined him all my life. I was disappointed. He spoke such weird German that I constantly had to ask what he'd said and he kept getting more and more impatient. And still, I really wanted him to like me. I wanted to show him that I was Jewish too. He never reacted to that.'

'But from then on you met regularly,' I said quickly, just in case Gabor wanted to make some caustic observation.

'Yes, perhaps every two or three months. I was also able to write to him, at a neutral address, because Lotte didn't want Marika to find out about me. But we stayed in contact until his death, even if sometimes there were long breaks in between. After he split up with Lotte and spent his last two years in the bosom of the Jewish community, we were even able to talk about Jewishness, but never about the past. I still remember giving him *The Gulag Archipelago* for his birthday, and how he threw it furiously on the floor and trampled on it. Never again did he want to read anything about any bloody camp, never again. I learned my lesson.'

There was a long pause. We heard the buzz of Hannah's mobile in her bag, vibrating three times in succession.

'And what was that about Holmes and Watson?' Gabor asked, looking at my mother.

'Oh no, I've just told it so many times,' she said. 'Maybe Lily would like to have a go. Sometimes I like to hear it from the outside.'

The story of how my mother learned of Hannah's existence is part of my basic repertoire, and it always hits the spot. There's a strictly factual, short version that's no less impressive for that, and a disco remix with a lot of embroidered details. Because I'd never told it in my mother's presence, I opted for the factual one, even though I knew I'd been given licence to elaborate, and my mother wouldn't interrupt unless I made some particularly silly mistakes.

'OK then. Mum used to go rummaging around in cupboards and drawers looking for answers. When she was about fourteen, on one of her forays she came across a letter. It was addressed to her father, and when she opened it a photograph fell out. The photograph showed a girl with red curly hair, more or less exactly the same age as her. And the accompanying letter began with the words 'Dear Dad'. For a moment my mother even thought she'd sent the letter herself. But then she worked out that this was the amazing discovery she'd been waiting for all her life, the kind that only ever happened to people in books. She waited until she was alone with Joschi, and demanded an explanation. Joschi's answer came so quickly, and was so well prepared, that even today Mum is convinced that he left the letter out specially for her as bait.'

'Every time we met, I bugged him about how much I would like to meet my sister,' Hannah interjected. 'I think he just felt beaten down.'

'Joschi said the letter was from his daughter Hannah,' I went on. 'Hannah lived with her mother, far away in another town, and she was exactly the same age as Marika – OK, a little bit younger, five months to be precise. Mum calculated and worked out that this was kind of a blow: Joschi had fathered another child before she was even born. But her enthusiasm at suddenly having a sister, after all the boring years of being an only child, and one who was still alive, was bigger than anything else, and shortly afterwards Joschi organized a meeting of the three of them.'

'Nice story,' said Gabor. 'I don't suppose I get a part in it too?'

'Afraid not,' said Hannah, 'unless Lily wants to put you in for dramatic reasons.'

For the time being I continued without Gabor. 'The first meeting took place in a zoo, just outside the monkey house. It was love at first sight, even though Hannah had brought my mother a record of Yiddish songs. Mum took her revenge the next time they met, when she forced Hannah to take drugs.'

'No, Lily, that's going too far,' said my mother. 'You should have seen the passion with which she dragged on that joint.'

'But I felt sick afterwards,' said Hannah. 'And I never touched the stuff again. And I don't want to know what you did with that brilliant record of mine.'

'You do show up in the story, Gabor,' said my mother. For our second meeting Hannah had actually planned to fill me in on absolutely everything. When the weekend was over, I was suddenly Jewish and had a brother called Gabor.'

'You just knew more about drugs than I did,' said Hannah.

'And about music.' My mother was a bit complacent in that regard.

'You found out from Hannah that I was your brother?' Gabor asked, surprised. 'And you hadn't had to listen to Auschwitz stories until then?'

'I grew up in Fairytale land, Gabor,' my mother replied. 'And Hannah in Jewish-children land. And you in no-man's-land.'

I wondered what sort of land I'd grown up in. I couldn't think of a name for it, but it was a benign and rather untidy land where people did an incredible amount of talking.

'Then, after that weekend, we had our big showdown,' my mother went on. 'Lotte was beside herself when she found out that Hannah had visited our flat. She forced Joschi to tell me that he was Gabor's father as well, and I pretended I was hearing it for the first time. In return I accused Joschi of never telling me that he was Jewish. And that was the end of Fairytale land. No more lies, but no truths either. It was almost another two years before Joschi moved out, but during that time we didn't get any closer, quite the contrary. I persuaded myself that I couldn't have cared less anyway.'

'There I can see a certain similarity between you and Gabor,' Hannah remarked. 'At least the couldn't-have-cared-less bit.'

'I was a punk, Doctor Hirschfeld,' replied my mother.

'Oh yeah, I forgot,' said Hannah and leant into me. 'She didn't even take the safety pin out of her ear at Joschi's funeral.'

'I'd never have got through that day without it. I was so furious that Joschi had simply pissed off. I was furious that hardly anyone there knew who Hannah was. And then there was that dreadful speech by the rabbi. I gave him all that information about Joschi, and he must have written it all down wrong.'

'But yours isn't true either,' said Gabor.

'Thanks for the memory, Gabor,' said Hannah. 'Where were you hanging out when Joschi was being buried? It would have been so nice, the three of us sitting there on the front pew in the cemetery chapel. Because you weren't there, I went and sat at the back instead, to spare Lotte's nerves. And I'd have stayed at the back if that punk woman there hadn't made such a fuss. No wonder the rabbi couldn't remember what he'd written down.'

'I was on holiday,' said Gabor. 'In Yugoslavia,' he added as if it explained everything.

We sat there for a moment longer without saying anything, and then my mother got up and set off in search of Anni to pay, while Hannah, eyes gleaming, studied the list of missed calls on her mobile. Gabor rubbed his fingers again, and I thought he made it really easy for a person to find him peculiar, and that I somehow liked him anyway.

'There's one more thing I'd like to know from you, if it's not too indiscreet,' he said suddenly to Hannah. 'Did you love Joschi? I mean, as a father – did you love him?'

My mother had come back and was standing motionlessly behind her chair, and I imagined that she was holding her breath.

Hannah looked as if she'd been taken completely by surprise. She snapped her phone shut and spent a long time rummaging in her handbag for a suitable place for it, before saying, 'No, sadly not. There was no one there. Or at least I could never get through to him.'

I knew she wasn't talking about phone calls, but I couldn't help seeing Hannah in front of me, sitting by one of those old-fashioned phones with a dial, trying over and over again to get through to Joschi. Then I remembered that there had actually been a scene like that many years ago. All I had to do was add my mother to the image, dialling Joschi's number from a different telephone, and then a third telephone that's constantly ringing. It's on a little table beside the wardrobe in the corridor, whose walls are hung with the same horrible seventies' wallpaper as the living room. On the shelf in front of the mirror there is a plain black yarmulke and a beautiful white one embroidered with silver threads. The phone won't stop ringing. It rings almost all day, until the startled caretaker finally opens the door to the flat with a second key. There lies Joschi, no more than a metre from the phone.

# *11*

WE DROVE THE FEW KILOMETRES to Weimar in silence. I was sitting in the back beside a Gabor who had become completely withdrawn again and was fiddling with his seat. If the four of us were going to go on another outing together, I would insist on swapping Gabor for my mother, but this time things weren't much cosier up in front. Perhaps it was because they'd been talking about love. Or about non-love. I thought about Jan.

We stopped at a pedestrian crossing. Through my window I saw a fat woman pushing a baby in a buggy hung with shopping bags with one hand, and with the other hitting the little boy who was walking along beside her. I guessed he was about eight years old. He was pretty over-weight as well. The bags were probably full of frozen pizza and hamburgers and sausages, and the boy had just told his mother that he was going to be a vegetarian from today, and only wanted to eat healthy things. And she had freaked out. She'd been quite irritable lately anyway because her boyfriend, the father of her youngest child, had left her the previous week for a nutrition adviser. I couldn't help thinking about Jan again.

When we got to the hotel, the scene of our arrival the previous day was played out all over again: a meeting point for the evening was agreed upon (eight o'clock in the lobby), and then everyone fled to their rooms. Because today no one bothered to give a reason for their with-drawal, things went even quicker than they had the previ-ous day. I took the lift up with my mother and noticed that she wanted to be alone. Wanting-to-be-alone was written, as usual, in neon on her forehead, but she still thought I wouldn't notice, and she's surprised and delighted that there's such a rapport between us every time I say I want to go off for a bit. The ritual then requires her to inquire with some concern about my plans, while the rest of her can hardly contain its yearning. This time, I think, it was a yearning for a long, quiet immersion in the tub. I planned to stay away for as long as possible.

Because I couldn't think of anything better to do, I headed towards the pedestrian zone, and the first thing I did when I got there was look around for the man with

the frying pan and the dog, but I couldn't see him anywhere. It had turned into a pleasant and relatively warm
afternoon. Most of the chairs at the pavement cafés were
full again, but my craving for caffeine had been more than
satisfied for today. Instead, I wanted to find a park, ideally
one with a park bench all to myself. And I was in luck:
two street corners on, I found a little children's playground with a sandpit, a slide and a swing, watched over
by a big chestnut tree, which was plainly seriously ill and
almost entirely bald. I couldn't help it, I immediately had
to baptize it the Goethe Chestnut. And of course, there in
the mild October sun the bench I'd wished for. Perfect.
But only nearly. There were two old people sitting on the
bench, a man and a woman, almost entirely hidden
behind their newspapers. Even without newspapers three
people wouldn't have fitted on the bench. Otherwise there
was no one to be seen. I felt a bit sorry for myself, and then
sat down on the edge of the sandpit. I could never quite
shake off the role of the child. The wood was still just a
little bit damp.

I took my notebook out of my rucksack and decided at
least to be a good child and work on my notes.

That's right: *Archive*, followed by three exclamation
marks. An application to the archive might clear every-
thing up all at once. *József Molnár, born on 19 October 1908.
Wait, here he is. Hungarian Jew, arrived September 1945.* Or:
*József Molnár? No, we can't find that name in our files.* Or:
*Yes, József Molnár is listed here as a political prisoner. Trade*

*unionist, Catholic.* I wasn't sure whether I wanted to be anywhere near Hannah when she found out.

Why had that important part of Joschi's past actually never been fully clarified? That was so typical of our family history: everyone operated on the basis of certain assumptions, but clearly no one really wanted to know. My mother and Hannah had agreed on one version and lived with it in their different ways, but now along came Gabor, the toy tester, and all of a sudden everything threatened to keel over again. In fact, all he had done was jiggle their stories around a tiny bit. A teddy-bear in his lab would probably have shaken it off quite easily, but it really seemed to have rattled Hannah. As if things weren't quite complicated enough already.

I stuck with my earlier working hypothesis, that my grandfather was Jewish. I thought of starting my essay with a few faked lines from Buchenwald, which he had written to his family from the camp, but then it occurred to me that my grandfather must have known what had happened to his wife in Hungary, and he didn't even know his other wives yet. It was a rotten idea anyway. I looked at the map of the camp again and drew in the route that I'd taken today. I flicked indecisively through the brochure and waited for inspiration to come. I scratched a random pattern in the sand and felt miserable. When I was just seriously starting to wonder whether I wasn't a born liar myself, my phone rang.

It was Jan. I saw his number on the display, and the first

thing I did was the thing I'd advised myself to do in all crisis situations: breathe. The ringtone grew louder. I looked at the couple on the bench. They didn't stir. Not even their newspapers moved. Perhaps they were a sculpture, and I'd fallen for it.

I cleared my throat and picked up my phone. 'Hello,' I said.

'Hey,' said Jan. 'Where are you? Can you talk? If not I'll call back later.'

No, not later. Later could mean having to run out in the middle of a heated debate between Gabor and Hannah, or even worse, getting back and having to face my mother's meaningfully raised eyebrows as she demanded a story. No, if at all, then now. 'I'm in a playground,' I said. 'All the other children are over seventy and they've left their hearing aids at home.'

The man on the bench lowered his paper and smiled at me benignly over the edge of it. I felt blood rushing into my face. Very funny, Lily.

'What did you say?'

'Oh, nothing,' I said. I didn't quite feel like dying, but I wasn't far off.

'How are you? How was Buchenwald?'

God, yes, Buchenwald. How many stories can you actually fit into a single day?

'I'm fine,' I said. 'And Buchenwald was . . . impressive.'

Because he didn't immediately reply, I added, '. . . and sad', but at that precise moment Jan said something to which we both asked at the same time, 'Sorry, what was that?', which nearly finished me off. I knew it would happen again as soon as I opened my mouth, so I said nothing and tried to concentrate on my breathing again and nearly suffocated.

'And how's your family reunion?'

'Brilliant. My uncle works in a lab that tests cuddly toys. He tortures them. But that way he saves little children.'

Jan hesitated for a moment, then he laughed. 'Sounds like an exciting uncle.'

For the first time I dared to look back towards the bench. The man had leaned sideways towards his wife, who was tapping at a spot in her newspaper, and looking at him expectantly. Perhaps they were reading the death notices together. Karl, my grandmother Lotte's second husband, had loved doing that as well, although he could never quite explain to me why he was so keen on it. All of a sudden I could easily imagine growing old with Jan and going to the playground every afternoon to read the paper, which assumed, however, our getting together in the first place. How do you explain to a thirty-year-old that a fourteen-year age difference doesn't really matter? I should ask my grandfather.

– *Joschi, was it a problem that Hannah's and Marika's mothers were so much younger than you?*

– *Was first not problem, then small problem and then very big problem.*

*– OK, I'll take Answer A.*
'Hello?' asked Jan. 'Are you still there?'
'Yes,' I said. 'It's a very exciting family generally.'
'I think so, too,' said Jan. 'How about we meet up for a coffee soon, and you tell me more about it?'
It didn't sound exactly like a proposal of marriage, but it did give me fresh hope.
'Sure,' I said. 'When?'
'Let's talk about it at school next week,' said Jan. My hope collapsed in on itself like a soufflé.
'OK, see you then,' I said, because I couldn't think of anything better.
'Take care of yourself, Lily,' said Jan, this time in his trainee-teacher voice.
I pressed the button, and his number, along with the length of the call (3 minutes 33 seconds) vanished from the display.

OK, then. No reason to panic. That call certainly wasn't one of the best in my life, but he had called me, and that wasn't part of his duties as a budding teacher of political geography. At least he had been delicate enough not to ask about the presentation I'd been so keen to do. I went through our conversation in my mind again, replacing my answers with remarkable statements like: (And how's your family reunion?) 'Brilliant. First we spent an hour meditating together, before talking about the effects of the Holocaust on the younger generation.' I did that until I reached the conclusion that nothing could actually have saved that conversation. That reconciled me to my own stammered speech. Of course I knew that trainee teachers get into trouble when they get involved with their pupils, and I didn't even really have to know Buddha's five *S las.* Perhaps Jan had one foot in jail already for religiously influencing his charges, because he'd taken me along to see his meditation teacher. Somehow things weren't looking good for us.

I went on staring for a while at the pattern by my feet and tried to use pure willpower to smooth the sand again. Then I realized it was time to leave the playground again. My path led me past the bench, and just in case I said a loud and clear 'Goodbye' when I drew level with the two old people. They looked up from their newspapers and nodded at me with faint bewilderment. They did so with almost perfect synchronization. I brushed some more sand off my trousers, took my leave of the sick Goethe Chestnut tree and left.

In the street I put on my headphones and opted to listen to Portishead, because I was so depressed and actually wanted to stay that way for a bit. In fact I didn't want to spend any more time walking around. I took an indecisive left turn, then a right turn, and then walked straight on for a while. Maybe I should go back to the hotel. Maybe I should switch schools or learn an instrument at last, the nose flute, for example. There was a whole pile of them in the shop window next to me. I'd mistaken them for wall-pegs or some sort of special dummy, but on the sign next to them it said quite clearly, 'Nose Flutes', and the very name was a gift. I took a closer look at the shop window. There were floating candles, a magical rose firework, a spider catcher that let you catch spiders alive without touching them, and an alarm clock on wheels that ran away after it went off. It was what a children's birthday party for grown-ups must be like. By the door was a box labelled 'Chinese sky lanterns – let your wishes rise to heaven. 10 for 35 Euros'. A picture showed hundreds of lanterns floating in the dark night sky.

The front door was ajar. I turned off my music and went into the shop. It was dimly lit. Behind the counter sat a girl reading a Manga comic.

'We're closed,' said the girl without looking up.

'I'd like to buy one of those wishing lanterns,' I said. 'Please, just this once.'

'They only come in packs of ten.' She snapped her comic shut and looked at me. She was Thai and about the same age as me – or perhaps ten years older, I couldn't tell. Her fringe was cut so straight that it looked like a black sweatband. 'For your party, yeah?'

'I can't afford ten,' I said. 'I really just need one.'

'Ten for 35 Euros,' she repeated. 'Extra special quality. Fly for at least ten minutes.'

'Can't you just sell me a single one?'

Haggling has never been one of my strong points. Neither has begging. Was I going to have to tell her my whole family history so that she would get the thing out of the box?

'Can't do it.' She tilted her head on one side and looked at me defiantly. 'One on its own is far too weak.'

She actually did want the story. 'OK then,' I said. 'You know the former concentration camp near here, Buchenwald?'

She nodded and didn't take her eyes off me.

'My grandfather was there. He was a Jew. His whole family was killed; he was the only one who survived. Tomorrow would have been his hundredth birthday. I'd like a lantern like that for him. I'd happily buy six million of the things off you, but unfortunately I only have enough money for one.'

'Oh,' she said. Then she thought for a moment. 'When I was putting the pack of lanterns away again a moment ago, there was one missing,' she said. 'I think it must have been stolen. I can't see everything all the time. No one can.'

'No, definitely not,' I said.

As we walked together to the door, she took a packet of lanterns and pressed it into my hand. 'The stuff about wishes is nonsense anyway,' she sad. 'The lanterns are actually for the dead, but that doesn't sell so well.'

'Thanks,' I said. 'Don't stolen things get taken out of your wages?'

She shook her head, but her fringe stayed exactly where it was. 'No problem.'

'Then I'd like to pay for at least the one,' I said, and thought I sounded just like my mother.

'Happy Birthday, Grandfather,' she said in English, and giggled. 'Ten lanterns is still ninety too few. All the very best.'

When I was back in the street, I heard the Manga girl locking the shop door behind me. I turned round and waved to her again. I didn't believe that the lanterns were really for the dead, but I thought it was nice of her to come up with that lie just for me. My mood was getting better and better. Perhaps my party was going to work after all.

# 12

THE DOOR TO OUR HOTEL ROOM was locked, but my mother had hung a 'Please Do Not Disturb' sign on the door handle and written 'I'm at Hannah's' across it. I put it in my pocket, because it said 'Please clean room' on the other side, and I'd always wanted a sign like that. Then I headed for the first floor.

Hannah pulled the door open as soon I knocked. She was wrapped in a big towel, and wore a second one on her head like a turban. Constructions like that don't last ten minutes when I make them, but Hannah's winding technique was perfect. She looked like a sixties' film-star, and her room resembled an artiste's wardrobe; whether before or after the performance, it was hard to say exactly. Even the obligatory bouquet was there, a grandiose spray of white lilies and dark red roses. They were in an ice bucket, and I don't think there would have been room for another single stem.

'This guy Edgar's an old poser!' my mother called out to me. She was sitting on the balustrade of Hannah's tiny balcony, just a few inches wide, and smoking.

'He's a true gentleman,' said Hannah, and ran her hand over a lily blossom.

I set the pack of lanterns and my rucksack down beside the door and carefully took a few blouses and scarves off the chair before I sat down.

'Your mother's just telling me why her company logo is a sheep with one of its ears bitten off. Do you know?' Hannah spun out of her towels like a temple dancer and threw them on the bed. Then she started getting dressed.

Of course I knew. 'The ear was chewed off by the Hungarian shepherd bear. Joschi gave Mum drawing lessons and told her that in Hungary they had bears who looked after the sheep.'

'Aren't family reunions wonderful?' Hannah exclaimed enthusiastically. 'You get to know each other better and learn things you didn't dare dream of.'

'For example, I've just discovered that you wear orange lace underwear,' said my mother, leaning forward for a better view while at the same time trying to leave her hand with the cigarette outside. It was exactly the kind of clumsy contortionism that she'd always tried to wean me off.

'Do you like it?' asked Hannah.

'Well, I think it's great,' I said.

'Me too, of course,' said my mother. 'But I'm a bit surprised that you're so taken aback by my sheep story.'

'I actually meant something else,' said Hannah, and pulled a bright yellow pullover out of the cupboard. 'I'm talking about Alfred's conspiracy theory, which Gabor presented us with today.' She stopped in the middle of the room and looked at my mother. 'I know it's completely nuts, but since he started on about it, part of my brain has been frantically looking for proof to contradict him. Do I need it? It's just bullshit even to claim Joschi wasn't a Jew!'

'And what if he wasn't?' asked my mother. 'Would it change anything?'

'Basically everything, yes,' said Hannah. And after a pause, 'It would actually be the worst thing that could happen to me.'

'Now you're being melodramatic,' said my mother.

'Oh, shut up,' said Hannah and climbed into a green woollen skirt.

'Would you rather be alone?' I asked, although I really didn't want to go.

'You just stay here, Lily,' said Hannah. 'Otherwise I might push your mother over the balcony.'

'If you get too noisy I can put my headphones on.' Like hell I would.

'I don't get you, Hannah,' said my mother, throwing her cigarette end into the street in a high arc. 'We go running up and down that horrible camp and afterwards you tell me the worst thing that could happen to you would be if our father wasn't a Jew and possibly wasn't even there?'

Hannah didn't reply. Instead her phone rang, no longer on silent this time. It wasn't film music or the Israeli national anthem – it sounded more like coughing. Hannah switched the phone off without even glancing at the display. It was the first time I'd seen her do such a thing. The situation was clearly serious.

'I stand by that,' she said. 'I'm not talking about war or violence; I'm talking about my own personal Chernobyl. I'm talking about my identity. Everyone has one. Or at least I hope they do. Mine is that I'm the daughter of a Jew and belong to that people, even if I don't satisfy the entrance requirements. I think the criteria have been selected very much at random, so I'm not convinced by them.'

'That doesn't matter a damn to any of them,' said my mother. 'Unless you convert. But you've always been too touchy to do that.'

'I'm not touchy, I'm an atheist,' said Hannah. 'I'd rather drop down dead than stand up there and read from the Talmud. Like lots of other Jews here and elsewhere. Damn it, I'm not concerned about the religion. I'm concerned about the people.'

'If you're not Jewish as far as Jews are concerned, and then it turns out that your father wasn't Jewish either, your situation hasn't changed in the slightest.' My mother was now operating in a way that only fascinated me when I wasn't in her crosshairs. 'What's the problem?'

'I'm the problem,' said Hannah. She went to the minibar, looked inside and slammed the door closed again with disgust. 'Shouldn't we be thinking about going downstairs?'

'In a minute,' said my mother. 'I want to know what you mean about your identity. You're still far more than the daughter of a Jewish father.'

'Like what?' Hannah put her hands on her hips and looked combatively at my mother. 'The daughter of an abandoned Catholic nurse? The accomplished bookseller specializing in Jewish literature? Jewish dating club member, success quota zero per cent so far?'

'Why not? Why, out of all the available possibilities, do you choose this one, when it doesn't get you anywhere anyway?'

'It gets me a whole lot, Marika,' said Hannah. 'And anyway, I've had enough time to get used to it. While you were drawing bears with Joschi, I was kneading little yellow stars out of Plasticine. You've just got two dead children on your wall at home, while in my books of photographs there were hundreds of them, and even today I can still remember all their faces. My people. If it was all a lie, *that* would be the worst thing for me.'

'But it wasn't Joschi who set you up as being Jewish.'

'No, that was my mother,' said Hannah. 'And you'll laugh, but nowadays I can even understand that. She couldn't give me a family, but she did give me a sense of belonging.'

'Belonging? She took the tragedy of Joschi's life and turned it into a giant fetish for you, I would say.'

It was like a game of tennis. My head wandered back and forth between the two of them, and with each new sentence I thought, yes, that's right.

'A giant fetish? You mean a huge great circumcised knob? Oh, why not,' said Hannah.

I sensed rather than saw my mother's frown, so I quickly cut in, 'I know what a knob is, Mum.'

'No, Hannah, I don't mean that,' said my mother and slipped back onto the floor from the balustrade of the balcony. 'I meant those wretched myths that flourish around Joschi. Let's be honest for once: what would Gabor's story, the story about your mother or Joschi's failed suicide attempt be without the Holocaust aftertaste. Just miserable little events. Everyday human failure. Even Joschi was far more than just a Jew who had lost his wife and children. He was an unsuccessful gambler, who didn't feel like having a job or a career. He was a seducer, and he was amazingly successful with women, even though he didn't look all that stunning. If no disasters showed up to destroy his relationships, he did it himself. We don't know if he was a great father to Tamás and Véra. We don't even know if he was still with his wife when she was deported to Auschwitz in 1944. We know nothing, nothing at all. We don't even have any tall tales from those days.'

'Does that surprise you?' asked Hannah. 'Eventually you're going to have to come to terms with the fact that there's no more information, and that's that. From that point onwards what matters is what you decide. For my part, I've made my decision.'

'Nice for you,' said my mother and dropped onto Hannah's bed. 'I haven't even made up my mind yet. So these speculations about whether Joschi mightn't have been a Jew leave me pretty cold. What a great story that would be! Joschi and Louise are sitting together at the kitchen table. Hey, Joschi, says Louise, this is a fantastic opportunity to get hold of some compensation. You were a forced labourer and then you were in a concentration camp. Your wife and children really did die in Auschwitz, after all. Come on, let's tell them you're a Jew – who's going to check, your papers have all disappeared anyway.'

For me it looked as if Holmes and Watson, for the first time in their history, were about to start investigating each other.

'Why are you starting on about all that again?' asked Hannah. 'Brilliant story, hah. I thought we'd agreed that we wouldn't have thought him capable of such a cynical strategy. And please get off my towels.'

'Our father wasn't a strategist, any more than you or I. He wouldn't have worked out his cock-and-bull story in advance; he'd have come up with it on the spur of the moment. "Enough shit, should pay for pain. Say I'm Jew." Something like that. And somehow,' said my mother, pulling Hannah's towels out from underneath her, 'I couldn't even blame him for that.'

I loved her very much at that moment, my odd mother, who could say great things and do strange ones at the same time.

'And I don't see that we've ever got to decide,' she went on. 'It's more that I think we should finally accept that it could have been like this, or it could have been like that. And make peace that way.'

'Amen,' said Hannah. I had a sense that she wasn't particularly impressed.

'When we were at Buchenwald, why didn't you ask whether they had documents about Joschi in their archive?' I asked her. 'You've been there before, and they give out information to everybody, don't they?'

Hannah stared at me for a while before she answered. 'I never doubted that he was there,' she said. 'What would I get from a sad list with his name on it? I know the documents that Marika has in her possession, but I wasn't even particularly interested in them. And the first time I visited Buchenwald I had enough to do just grasping the sheer monstrosity of it all: that such a place even existed, less than ten kilometres from here.'

'After the liberation, the Americans sent the inhabitants of Weimar to the camp to see what had been going on

outside their front door for years.' At least I could con-
tribute a bit of information from the brochure.

'Yes,' said Hannah. 'I've seen photographs of those
visits. Some of the people look really shocked, but far too
many faces are saying: what's all this got to do with *me*?'

'Are there any faces in old photographs that you
haven't noticed?'

'No,' said Hannah, and there wasn't a hint of doubt in
her voice.

At that moment there was a knock at the door. It was a
quiet, hesitant knock, but we all still gave a start.

'Shit, it's ten to nine,' said my mother, leaping up from
the bed. 'We'd arranged to meet at eight down in the
lobby.'

'I'll get it,' I said, and went to the door.

Of course it was Gabor. He was carrying a full paper
bag in each hand and looked a bit stressed out.

'I've been shopping,' he said. 'I didn't think any of you
would want to spend another evening in the pub.'

'Oh great,' I said and stepped aside. Gabor took a few
steps into the room and held up his bags as if to prove once
again that he was unarmed and had come on a peaceful
mission.

'Could I maybe put these ...'

'Just a moment,' said Hannah, taking the ice bucket
with Edgar's flowers off the table and, after thinking for a
moment, carting it into the bathroom.

'Great idea,' said my mother. It sounded as if she was talking about Gabor's groceries, but I think in fact she was particularly glad that she was saved from the sight of Edgar's monster bouquet.

Gabor set his bags down and started unpacking them. 'I didn't know whether you'd want to be on your own,' he said. 'But then I thought . . .'

'We didn't,' said Hannah. 'We just didn't notice the time. Sorry.'

'It's fine, this way I was able to make myself a bit useful,' Gabor replied and set two bottles of red wine down on the table. After these came two bottles of water and then the obligatory children's Coke, just for me. I don't like Coke. But at the sight of some baguette sandwiches my mouth started watering.

'You like this kind of stuff, right?' Gabor asked, almost happily.

I saw my mother and Hannah exchanging glances. I knew my mother's, it meant: don't you dare start this argument again. Hannah's glance was accompanied by a beaming smile and raised the anxiety that Watson had no intention of following Holmes' instructions.

'I mean, so far I haven't yet contributed much to our family party,' Gabor went on, and upended the second paper bag so that a set of plastic forks and knives rained down on the sandwiches, followed by napkins. Then he carefully folded both bags together until they looked like perfect little squares.

'So, erm . . .' he said.

Suddenly we all leapt into action at the same time. My mother opened the wine bottle with a rattly corkscrew that came with the room, while Hannah complemented the two drinking glasses with two tooth mugs from the bathroom and I arranged the sandwiches on a spread-out napkin. What the knives and forks were for remained unclear. Hannah offered Gabor the only other chair in the room to perch on, while she herself sat down in the armchair. My mother sat on the edge of the bed and poured out wine, and I squatted on the floor.

'Not for me, please, I'd rather have some water,' said Gabor. 'I actually only drink a glass of wine once a year at most. I don't know yet if this is the day.'

'It's the other way around with me,' said Hannah. 'I know *exactly* that this isn't the day I'm not going have one.'

'Cheers, then,' said my mother.

'Happiness to all living creatures,' I added and raised my glass of water.

'L'Chaim,' said Hannah emphatically.

For a while we sat peacefully side by side and ate our sandwiches. Or, put it like this, it was as peaceful as it could be, if you knew that Hannah still had an ace somewhere up her sleeve.

'And?' asked Gabor, carefully wiping a few crumbs from his trousers and catching them just as conscientiously with his other hand. 'Have you gained any additional knowledge about our father?'

'We're leaving the research up to Lily from now on, and refraining from any further speculation,' said my mother, sounding very determined.

'But why?' Hannah's eyes sparkled with enthusiasm. 'Lily will deal with the archive, that much is clear. But I see one other possibility that I would like to pursue.'

'And that would be?' Anything that prompted enthusiasm in Hannah put my mother in a state of high alert. Gabor, too, lowered his sandwich, from which he had taken a bite, and looked suspiciously at Hannah.

'Oh, just a small thing really,' said Hannah, and gave Gabor her loveliest smile. 'Would you be so kind as to give me a sample of your saliva?'

# 13

GABOR BLINKED WITH DISBELIEF. My mother rolled her eyes. No one said anything. I considered it highly unlikely that Hannah wanted to expose Gabor as a serial killer or perform a paternity test on him, but no other possible uses of saliva tests occurred to me for the time being. My mother looked as if she knew a few, but would prefer not to talk about them.

'There's nothing disgusting about it at all,' Hannah said. 'I read an article about it a while ago, and then did some research on the internet. There are private institutions that can run genetic tests on you to tell you where your ancestors came from and whether they were Jewish.

They compare your results with other DNA profiles from their database, and if you're lucky they can even find people you're related to – all over the world.'

'Forget it,' said Gabor.

'Hannah, this is ridiculous,' said my mother.

Hannah would not be diverted. 'Gabor, you're the only person in the world, as far as we know, running about with a copy of Joschi's Y chromosome. My own genetic analysis only lets me explore the maternal line. Come on, go along with this a bit. And I can keep the results secret if you don't want to know.'

'No,' said Gabor, keeping a close eye on the water glass from which he had just been drinking.

'Why not?'

'Because I've had enough bother with my father's lousy genes already, if you really want to know.'

It was all my mother could do to keep quiet.

'Gabor,' Hannah said soothingly. 'None of us would deny that you had more trouble with Joschi than anyone else. But to suggest now that his genes are responsible for your quality of life seems to be going a little too far.'

'Hannah,' Gabor replied, imitating Hannah's cadence. 'I'm not talking about my screwed-up childhood, OK?'

'What are you talking about, then?'

'I just don't want to know, that's all.'

'But what did you mean about your lousy genes? Is your baldness such a problem?'

'Hannah, just stop now,' said my mother.

Gabor sighed. Then he said, 'I'm sick.'

'What sort of sick?' asked my mother. I think she was so glad of the unexpected switch of subject that she would have been willing to listen to case histories for hours on end. My mother says she can't deal with illness, her own or anyone else's. I can confirm that. When I'm ill she treats me with food, homoeopathy, enough reading material and a telephone within reach, so that I can feel sorry for myself somewhere else. It's worked pretty well so far.

'Haemochromatosis.' Gabor squeezed the word out like the last bit of toothpaste from the tube.

'Never heard of it,' said my mother.

'Hardly anyone has, but it's one of the commonest genetic diseases in this part of the world.'

In my head I ran through my foreign vocabulary and worked out something like brightly coloured blood, but it could hardly be that.

'Do we have it too?' asked Hannah.

'In all likelihood you don't. It takes two people who have the same defective gene but don't have the illness themselves. Joschi and Louise were the dream couple in that respect.'

In my mind's eye I saw the illustrations from my biology textbook: Mendelian pea flowers and inherited haemophilia.

'Are you some sort of haemophiliac, Gabor?' I asked, even though I hadn't really wanted to get involved in this conversation.

'No, Lily, the other way around,' said Gabor. 'I just have to have half a litre of blood drained once or twice a month. If I didn't, there'd soon be so much iron in my organs and joints that you could pick me up with a magnet.'

I presume that was supposed to be a child-friendly explanation for me, but I still found it oddly menacing. I remembered Gabor rubbing his fingers in the car and later in the café.

'Does it hurt?' said my mother, as matter of fact as ever. Soon she'd be fetching a telephone.

'Yes, but you get used to it. I got the diagnosis twenty years ago, but it took them almost five years to work it out. For a long time they assumed I was an alcoholic because my liver results were so bad. That was the obvious leap to make, because there was an alcohol problem in the family anyway. Eventually it occurred to somebody to do a genetic test. Since then the thing has a name, and quite a nice one at that.'

Gabor laughed his strange laugh, and I calculated how much blood they must have tapped over the past twenty years. I saw a row of litre bottles, almost forty metres long.

'Hang on,' said Hannah. 'I can't always get my head around the notion of illnesses. You say Joschi and Louise had the same defective gene?'

'That's not as weird as it sounds,' said Gabor.

'You mean Joschi knew about it?'

'Unlikely,' said Gabor. 'Or did you think we might

have found an explanation for why he chose a new woman for each of his children?'

'What nonsense,' said Hannah, but she looked slightly embarrassed.

'It sounds more dramatic than it really is.' Gabor took the water bottle and filled his glass. 'The pains in my joints are the worst problem. Luckily my liver has recovered. The only effective therapy for this illness is regular bloodletting. Being reminded of my parents' unhappy relationship twice a month is just about bearable. If I don't forget to do it, my life expectancy is exactly the same as any other chain-smoker.'

Hannah looked at Gabor for a while, and then nodded. 'OK. Sorry if you thought you'd been ambushed,' she said. 'For me the one thing has nothing to do with the other, but now I understand why you mightn't be keen on genetic tests. Fine, let's just leave it at that.'

I imagined Gabor with a cannula in his arm, lying on a hospital couch, seeing his blood flowing out and thinking about Joschi and Louise. Then I remembered Joschi's claim about having blue blood in his veins. I don't know why, but it made me sad.

'Thanks for your understanding,' said Gabor.

We said nothing and went on eating and drinking, but it wasn't an unfriendly silence. Eventually my mother went into the bathroom and immediately came shooting out again and said the bathroom was unusable, and that Edgar's lilies were a violation of the narcotics laws.

Hannah stayed completely cool, and just said she was really looking forward to introducing Edgar in person to my mother in the near future, and warned her to brace herself for his aftershave.

Gabor went to the balcony and leaned far over the balustrade and smoked a cigarette. I went too, and stood beside him because I wanted to see what the weather was like and know something about Gabor. At least it wasn't raining.

'No,' Gabor said in reply to my question. 'I have no family. And I never wanted one either.'

'What are you talking about out there?' my mother called.

'All I've got is my record collection,' said Gabor contentedly, almost tenderly. 'If I was as young as you I'd probably have my Walkman on all the time as well. Although I actually think you shouldn't take music with you, you should go to it.'

He actually did say 'Walkman', but the correct term wouldn't have suited him, either. There he was at last, generation of '68. He was probably one of those freaks whose flats were empty but for a high-end amplifier with a record player that no one else was ever allowed to go near – next to enormous speakers with copper cables as thick as your arm growing out of them.

'Maybe I'll pay you a visit some time,' I said, and was shocked at the boldness of my approach, but Gabor just nodded enthusiastically and threw his cigarette end over the edge with exactly the same gusto as my mother had done a little while before.

'I've got a question for you,' said Gabor when we were sitting in Hannah's room again. 'There's a story that Louise only gave strange hints about, but never really came out with. What I managed to gather from it was that just before Marika was born Joschi had a serious accident. Do you know anything more about that?'

'Accident is good,' said Hannah, and set about opening the second bottle of wine.

'Are you serious?' asked my mother. 'You don't know that story? It's one of the best, and it's still 80 per cent true.'

'Eight-five per cent,' Hannah corrected her.

'Joschi and Lotte had a weekend relationship until I was born,' said my mother. 'They'd been married for two years, but somehow they'd never quite got round to moving in together. About four weeks before the due date, Lotte got a letter from Joschi. It was a farewell letter. He wrote that he would already be dead by the time she read his lines. That he loved her and that he was terribly sorry. You know, the sort of thing you write in a letter like that. Lotte dropped everything, ran to her neighbour, who had a telephone, and called Louise.'

I knew the story very well. I actually thought it was one of the strangest and saddest Joschi stories, but when my mother and Hannah told it together, it suddenly got bizarre and in places even funny. Then I always thought, yes, of course, it's a story about a survivor, isn't it?

'My mother and I were standing with similar letters in their hands at exactly the same time,' said Hannah, who had finally got the bottle open. 'Just a few days previously she'd met Joschi and told him the happy news that she was expecting a child by him. Hmm, and now something like this. She dropped everything too, ran to her neighbour, who had a telephone, and phoned Louise.'

'Why Louise? Did your mother know Louise?'

'They weren't exactly friends, but they were in contact. I assume Louise was the only one who knew about Joschi's triangular affairs.' Hannah poured wine for herself and my mother. Gabor thought for a while and then held out his glass as well. So it was his day after all. I said no thanks, but no one was interested.

'Are we really still within the 85 per cent truth zone?' asked Gabor. He looked very composed, almost solemn, as he took the first sip from his glass.

'Quite definitely,' said my mother. 'So, the phone was always ringing at Louise's, but she wasn't particularly surprised by that; after all, she had received a letter herself. And Louise didn't just have a telephone, she lived in the same city as Joschi. She phoned all the hospitals until at last she found the hospital to which Joschi had been admitted after his suicide attempt.'

'Let me guess,' said Gabor. 'He'd won a pistol in a poker game, but he'd missed.'

Of course, it must have been the red wine. For the first time I heard Gabor saying something that sounded vaguely like the start of a story.

'Wrong. Sleeping tablets,' said my mother.

'And of course not enough,' Hannah added. 'But so it was that all three of our mothers met for the first and last time in their lives. Like a scene in a film: three women, two of them pregnant, a failed suicide, a hospital bed. At this point, however, all 85 per cent of truth is used up. All we know is the results from this encounter. My mother, who insisted firmly until she died that she hadn't known Joschi had been married for two years, completely severed contact with him.'

'And Lotte and Joschi finally came to terms with the situation, but their marriage was over before it had really begun,' said my mother.

'My God, what a story,' said Gabor. 'And what about the other 15 per cent?'

'That's for speculation about what happened during the meeting,' said Hannah. 'To do with as we like.'

'Unfortunately my imagination doesn't run to that,' Gabor said regretfully.

'Hey, why don't we just re-enact the whole thing?' cried my mother, jumping up so impetuously that her wine glass almost tipped over. 'After all, we're the ideal cast for something like this. Come on, Lily, you lie on the bed and be Joschi.'

'I don't want to be Joschi,' I said furiously.

'Then Gabor's Joschi. That's much better, in fact.' When my mother had a bee in her bonnet, no one and nothing could stop her. 'Lily's Louise, Hannah is Frieda and I'm Lotte. Come on Gabor, onto the bed with you. You may not be feeling very well, you've just had your stomach pumped. We're in 1959, and you've got yourself into a pretty dreadful situation.'

As long as I live I will always be amazed that Gabor actually joined in. Perhaps he thought he owed the family a favour after refusing the saliva sample. Perhaps it was the wine, too, doing something to his Y chromosome. At any rate he stood up, lay down on his back on the bed and asked, 'Now what?'

'Oh no, Marika,' Hannah said. 'Does it have to be like this?'

'You're to be spared nothing, my dear Frieda,' said my mother, looking almost like Lotte.

'For God's sake,' Hannah replied. She took a few deep breaths. Then she walked to the bed and shouted, 'Joschi, does this mean that it was all a lie – our love and our dream of a future together? Why did you keep putting me off, and why did you keep everything else from me?'

Gabor blinked violently. He plainly couldn't think of an answer, but what could anyone have said to that?

'I've always trusted you, Joschi.' Now it was my mother's turn. 'I've never asked you what you got up to when we were not together. I thought you were looking

forward to having a family as much as I was. I thought
you were looking for a decent job. I thought ...'

'I thought I was the only one who could heal your
broken heart,' Hannah interjected.

'No, that's me, of course,' said my mother.

I had a feeling there wasn't much in the script for
Louise at this point, so I stayed out of it for the time being.

'I wanted a child with you, so that you'd finally make
your mind up,' said Hannah.

'Erm ... OK – I've always told you that I didn't want
any more children.' All of a sudden Gabor came to life.
'Children need a father, and not an, erm ... not a ghost.
Exactly, that's it. I'm a ghost! A ghost!'

'*I* didn't marry a ghost,' my mother said defiantly.

'No. No, you have a vampire for a husband,' Gabor
replied. 'I'm addicted to your beauty and your *joie de vivre*.
I've betrayed you. I've betrayed Frieda. I have every
reason to kill myself.'

'OK, OK,' I said as Louise, because I thought it was
time for me to say something.

'You have absolutely no reason to kill yourself,' said
my mother. 'You've just fathered another child, so just
be careful.' She paused for a moment and then said,
'No, that wasn't Lotte just then, that was me. Lotte would
have said: But suicide is never a way out, Joschi. We can
find a solution to any problem just as long as we stay
together!'

'Then I'd better go,' said Hannah resignedly.

I wanted to call out to Gabor to tell her to stay, to say he was looking forward to their child, but I was afraid I would change the course of history by doing so. I also wanted my mother and Hannah, standing along the long side of the bed as Lotte and Frieda, to look at each other at last and like each other, but even that seemed to be ruled out by future developments. But above all I wanted Louise to make a reasonable contribution to the advance of world history. Bugger the space–time continuum.

'OK, listen,' I said. 'Before we do anything else, shouldn't we be glad that Joschi survived?'

Three faces stared at me in shock. I silently begged Louise for forgiveness and said the first thing that came into my head.

'Perhaps none of this is salvageable, but I don't think our children should suffer as a result. Somehow they belong together. I'm sure Gabor would be glad to have two little sisters. He's so lonely.'

'But then your whole adoption story falls apart, Louise darling,' said Hannah.

'So?' I said. 'Enough secrets. If Joschi won't tell us anything about his time in the war, that's his business. But our children should know who they are and where they come from. And be proud of it.'

*And get up and tell their children*, I thought. If my Louise wanted to let it all out without regard for the consequences, at least it was happening because I wanted it to.

Gabor had sat halfway up in the middle of the bed, and was struggling to speak.

'Erm, Louise,' he croaked. 'Look, I don't know what to say . . .'

'Then just leave it,' my mother said softly.

'Yes, Joschi, just shut up,' said Hannah. 'Maybe I'll meet up with Lotte and Louise later on, and we can talk about it in peace.'

Who knows what could have become of our 15 per cent of uncertainty if a beeping sound hadn't suddenly started coming from beside the bed, first slowly, then faster and faster and with mounting volume. Gabor looked around wildly.

Hannah leapt over to the bedside table and switched off the alarm clock. 'Still ten minutes till midnight,' she exclaimed. 'Get out the Sekt, children! We're nearly ready.'

'I have another suggestion,' I said.

# 14

WE LEFT THE HOTEL at about half past one in the morning.
In the boot of our car there was a bottle of sparkling
wine, my pack of ten Chinese lanterns and Edgar's
bouquet. Its fragrance gave my mother such violent asth-
ma-like attacks every time we reached a junction, which
Hannah acknowledged with great satisfaction, given that
my mother was the one who had fetched the bouquet out
of the bathroom with the words 'Edgar's coming too!',
and brought it along in spite of Hannah's violent protests.
My wish for a new seating arrangement had – at least par-
tially – been answered: Gabor, the only one still capable of
driving, was at the wheel; Holmes and Watson were

reconciled and giggling on the back seat; and, armed with my map of the camp and a torch, I was sitting beside Gabor as usual. But this time I was fine with it.

It had turned cold and the starry sky was almost clear. The moon, caught on the wane and already visibly dented on the right-hand side, was pale and high in the sky.

'Gabor?' I asked him quietly because I didn't feel like embarking on a lengthy discussion. 'Was Alfred actually a Nazi?'

'I've often wondered that myself,' said Gabor.

The conversation on the backseat suddenly fell silent. I should have known.

'Does that mean you've never talked about those things, or what?' I said.

We had left the city boundary of Weimar behind us. So far we hadn't met a single car. The forest was edging closer. Soon the obelisk would appear and send us down the Blood Road.

Gabor shook his head. 'No, never. And you can be certain that I provoked him endlessly, but he never admitted anything of the kind. Any more than he denied it.'

'And what do you think?' My mother's head appeared between the front seats.

'I don't think he was a Nazi,' said Gabor. 'I could even imagine him having been a Party member, but he was an officer in the Wehrmacht, not an SS man. An ultra-conservative opportunist, who was incredibly ashamed after the war, but not even he could admit it afterwards.'

'Yes, that's what I think too,' said my mother and fell back against her chair. 'However horrific I might have found him, he didn't strike me as a Nazi. Not even a reformed Nazi.'

'I'm glad of that,' I said.

A car behind approached us with great speed and overtook us. A few moments later we reached the Buchenwald turn off.

I had been amazed by how little persuasion it had taken for the others to join in with my plan to drive back to the memorial and set off a Chinese lantern for Joschi, thanks be to the red wine. I was sure my mother had enough criminal energy to approve of an illegal nocturnal trespass of the camp grounds, as long as it was in honour of Joschi. Some practical and entirely justified objections had been raised by Hannah ('There are bound to be guards around the place. And I'm sure they'll have video cameras installed, too.'), but once my mother had suggested simply seeing the whole thing as an athletic challenge, particularly as we were travelling as a patrilineal Jewish delegation on a peace mission, she agreed and immersed herself in the instruction guide for the Chinese lanterns. But what I had never expected in my wildest dreams was Gabor's enthusiasm, and, even more than that, his scouting knowledge. Apparently, on his forays through the small camp the previous morning, he had discovered, more or less by chance, a path through the forest that led outside, running along the edge of the wood for a while and then suddenly stopping at a main road to the north of the camp. As we established with the help of my map, that road could only be a continuation of the Blood Road that led past the camp grounds to the neighbouring village.

A car came towards us and only dipped its headlights when it was almost level with us. Gabor cursed. I watched after the lurching headlights and wondered if only idiots were out and about at that time of night. Then I thought that most people would probably think of us as idiots as well.

'You're cursing in Hungarian,' my mother observed.

'That's not Hungarian, it's Serbian,' Gabor replied.

'But Joschi used exactly those words. I always thought they sounded stupid, so I didn't want to copy them. But I was sure they were Hungarian curses.'

'Joschi cursed in Serbian because he was a Jewish forced labourer in Yugoslavia,' Hannah cut in. 'It'll all be used at the evidentiary hearing. Ha!'

'What was that thing about *pichka*?' I asked. Gabor pretended not to have heard. 'And actually why did Joschi never really learn German?'

'Passive resistance!' cried Hannah.

'Perhaps he just wasn't very good at languages,' said my mother.

'But he once told me he spoke fluent French,' Hannah protested.

'*Faîtes vos jeux*, exactly,' said my mother, and then they both laughed.

We passed the turn off with the belltower. It couldn't be long now before we reached the memorial car park. I realized that I was gradually getting more nervous. The time when I had felt safe simply because I was in the company of adults seemed to have passed. Perhaps this was the end of my childhood. I found the moment entirely appropriate. I'm sure Joschi did too. *How my granddaughter grew up on way to small camp*, I could just imagine him telling that story.

The road bent sharply to the left. Buchenwald Station platforms must have been somewhere on our right. I'd only seen them from the car on yesterday's outing. There wouldn't have been five platforms – two or three would obviously have been enough.

'I'm going to drive past the car parks at a quite normal speed, and then I'll keep going. So we don't draw the attention of any guards that might happen to be there.'

'You're doing brilliantly, Gabor,' said Hannah. 'If you'd just quickly take my number plates off my happiness would be complete.'

'We can do that afterwards, in case we have to escape by car,' said my mother. 'We haven't done anything yet. I haven't even got any dope on me.'

'That's a shame,' said Hannah. 'For the first time in all those years I quite fancy some.'

We passed the entrance to the car parks, flanked by the yellow barrack buildings. Then the forest swallowed us up again. According to my map, on our right was the part of the camp where the SS had built their stables and their riding arena, and where they had later shot Soviet prisoners of war. Even deeper into the forest lay the actual prisoner-of-war camp with its watchtowers and barbed wire fences, most of which had long ago turned to rust and no longer represented an obstacle.

'Soon we should be level with the Small Camp,' said Gabor. 'Right, Lily?'

'Right,' I said, after glancing at the map. 'And it's not far from here to the place where we were going to get out.'

A car came towards us. I had to struggle not to throw myself sideways when the headlights caught me. Behind me I heard my mother and Hannah having similar impulses. Gabor laughed out loud. The car drove past us and didn't even slow down. I could make out two people in it.

'How come you're actually so damned cool?' Hannah shouted from the back seat.

Gabor laughed again. 'I'm enjoying this,' he said.

Then I started enjoying it too.

Shortly afterwards the patch of woodland ended on the left. From here the main road ran straight between fields and gentle hills to the next village. Gabor braked and then turned right off the road. What I had at first thought was a little path through the fields proved after only a few metres to be a cul-de-sac. Gabor guided the car as far as he could into the undergrowth. Then he switched the engine off and turned the lights out. Suddenly it was pitch-black and silent.

'So, ladies, according to our plan we now have two possibilities,' said Gabor. 'We could head off to the right through the bushes and trust that we'll somehow get through. If we stay more or less in the right direction we should be in the Small Camp in about half a kilometre.'

'What was the second one?' asked Hannah.

'That's the night walk. It would involve a bit of a detour, but for most of the way we could stay on the path that I walked along yesterday. The advantage would be that I know my way a bit.'

'I'm in favour of the night walk,' said my mother. We all agreed on this. And on turning on the torch as little as possible, and on taking our plan to its conclusion even if it was going to be difficult or risky (my wish), and not going wandering off on our own (my mother's wish, probably referring to me). We checked that our car couldn't be seen by chance from the road. Then we set off, a strange expedition moving along the edge of the forest: at its head Gabor, carrying the pack of lanterns, whose progress could, in case of emergency, have been followed by his cigarette smoke; then me with Edgar's bouquet; behind me, Hannah with the bottle of Sekt; and last of all my mother with the task of keeping a lookout. I was disappointed by how little light such a pale moon produced, but at least in this darkness we were better protected against discovery. We stumbled over branches and stepped in puddles, but no one complained. Two cars passed each other on the main road and then disappeared again, as we walked about 300 metres in single file, before we reached the spot where Gabor had stood the day before.

'And now?' asked my mother.

'First left and then right again,' said Gabor. 'This is the chain of sentry posts leading all the way around the camp grounds. Now we're going to walk all the way along the old border fence.'

By now our path could no longer be seen from the road, so I could turn the torch on every now and again. Concrete posts protruded from the ground at regular intervals on the right-hand side. They were in various stages of dilapidation. Some of them still looked completely intact, others had collapsed in on themselves, and their rusty innards stuck out like springs. I couldn't see any barbed wire anywhere.

'It's horrible here,' said my mother. 'I always imagined that all the dead and all that misery would have just left peace behind. But what still hangs in the air here is this intangible malevolence.'

'Then Lily's idea of the Chinese lanterns is quite right,' Gabor replied. I could almost have hugged him. I did so in my mind, and then concentrated on counting the paces between the posts again: sometimes it was six, sometimes seven. I was slightly surprised to find that the German camp architects hadn't been all that precise about their distances.

'Shush for a minute,' Hannah said suddenly and paused. There was the sound of an engine in the distance.

It wasn't coming from the road, which was already far behind us. It was coming from the right, from the direction of the camp. We pricked up our ears to hear if it was coming closer, but after a while it fell silent again.

'It's actually reassuring to know that there are guards out and about,' said Hannah.

'Let's hope that they can tell good trespassers from bad ones,' said my mother. 'I hope you realize that they're guaranteed to find us?'

'But only when we've finished,' I said. I was cold, I was tired – but I felt great. I wanted to spread confidence and decisiveness and nothing else. I was starting to enjoy the end of my childhood more and more. I also found the fact that it coincided with my grandfather's hundredth birthday highly pertinent in case anyone asked me about it afterwards.

We marched on. About ten minutes later we reached a patch of open ground, surrounded by a chain-link fence. Inside there were several small brick buildings connected by walkways.

'The sewage works,' said Gabor. 'Not far now. We have to turn right.'

'But there's no path here,' said my mother.

'We'll just walk along the fence and then through the undergrowth for a bit,' Gabor explained.

'Oh, brilliant,' said Hannah. 'The effect of the wine is waning, by the way. I can actually feel myself getting more and more cowardly.'

'At any rate, it's better if you're more sober again,' said my mother. 'You're the only one who's read the instructions for the lanterns.'

Gabor turned right, and we followed him. Even though I tried really hard, I couldn't help Edgar's bouquet shedding a few lily-flowers in the bushes. Somewhere in one of the brochures I'd read that the Small Camp had been neglected for a long time after the war. By the time it was made accessible again, the forest had long ago reclaimed its territory. That meant the trees here must have all have been as old as Gabor. I told him so. He didn't reply, but I sensed that he was smiling.

A few minutes later Hannah decided we were at our destination. We had reached a little clearing, and Gabor estimated that we were less than a hundred metres away from the memorial to the Small Camp, which meant that we were also very close to the open area with the barrack foundations. For a moment my mother broke her own rules and stalked off to verify Gabor's information. She stayed away for exactly as long as it took Hannah and me to spread the ten lanterns out on the ground in front of us and open the Sekt – just to be on the safe side. Gabor sat on a tree stump and smoked. I was impressed at how silently my mother could move in the dark.

'Everything is just as Gabor said,' she whispered. 'It's not far from here to the camp proper, but I don't think anyone can see us from there. There's some light coming from the administration block, and from the gate building and the two watchtowers as well, but all in all it's pretty dark out there.'

'Why are you suddenly whispering?' Hannah asked.

'Because I could hear your voice from quite a long way away,' said my mother, now speaking at normal volume. 'OK, let's get going. Which of the lanterns is for Joschi?'

It wasn't until the next day that she told me she'd seen the guards' van in the distance behind the gate building. We'd already got that far. Why spread panic unnecessarily? The main thing was that Joschi would finally be able to fly.

# *15*

GABOR HAD STUBBED OUT HIS cigarette and sat down next to us. At our feet lay the folded-up lanterns. They glowed in the darkness.

'So, which one's for Joschi?' my mother repeated. 'And what's going to happen to the other nine?'

'We've got just enough dead,' said Hannah. 'I've worked it out. You won't believe it, but it's exactly ten.'

We said nothing. We were all counting in our heads.

'Is Alfred on your list, for example?' Gabor sounded surprised.

'Of course,' said Hannah. 'Or are you going to say he didn't play a part in Joschi's life?'

'Karl didn't know Joschi, but I think it's good if he's there,' I said.

'Karl fits in 100 per cent,' my mother replied. 'He was very happy with Lotte, and took over Joschi's job as grandfather.'

'Good, then that's that one sorted,' said Hannah. 'One for Joschi, five for his wives, two for Tamás and Véra, two for Karl and Alfred. It said in the instructions that it takes two people to set off the lanterns. One holds it at the top, the other one lights the flame. Then you have to wait a while until the air has warmed up enough and is pulling upwards, and then you let go.'

'How long do the things actually stay in the air?' Gabor asked.

'About ten or fifteen minutes. They can fly up to four hundred metres. Then eventually the flame goes out, and they fall back to earth like little parachutes. At least that's what it says in the instructions.'

I crouched on the ground and carefully pulled one of the lanterns apart. It was about fifty centimetres in diameter and about one metre long; it was made of thin rice paper and looked like a cross between a shopping bag and a baker's hat. It was stabilized at the base by a thin wire ring, at the middle of which was a flat container containing solid fuel. The paper felt delicate and light as a feather in my hands.

'This one's for Joschi,' I said. 'Shall we make it fly now?'

'I'd like to light it,' said Gabor.

'Yes, you two do that,' said Hannah.

I lifted the lantern with both hands by the very tips, as high as I could. Gabor held the flame of his lighter to the fuel. It immediately flickered into life. It smelled of alcohol. The paper shell began to inflate.

'Hey, Joschi,' said my mother. 'Not like travelling from Platform 5 all the time, is it?'

It went much faster than I'd expected. The lantern had completely unfolded by now, its paper seams were rigidly tensed. The rice paper almost touched my face, and I could feel the warm air from inside on my skin. I reached with one hand for the ring at the bottom and became aware of a gentle upward pull, as if from a helium balloon.

'I think I'll be able to let go in a second,' I said.

The pull became stronger. Now I was holding the lantern by the bottom with both hands. As soon as I relaxed my grip slightly, it started pushing its way upwards.

'Watch out,' I said.

I opened my hands and moved them aside. For two or three seconds Joschi's lantern hung motionlessly in the air, as if thinking about its route. Then it started rising vertically into the night sky, as if someone were pulling it up from above on a line. There was something sublime, something majestic about it. I felt like applauding. From below, the lantern looked like a glowing, fiery eye.

'Bon voyage, Joschi,' said my mother.

'We're thinking of you,' said Hannah.

Gabor cleared his throat twice before he said, 'It was nice getting to know you a bit better.'

'And, by the way, you owe this party to your grand-daughter!' my mother called after it, under her breath.

'And the bouquet's from Edgar,' Hannah added.

'All the best for your birthday, Joschi,' I said, and silent-ly added, 'I'm proud you're my grandfather,' but that con-cerned only me and Joschi.

For a while we watched Joschi's light in silence. Hannah looked in the dark for the Sekt bottle and knocked it over, but there was enough left for us to drink to Joschi's last journey. My mother refused to make a speech, even though Gabor and Hannah asked her to several times. Instead she urged us to keep going. It was not even ques-tioned that the next round would go to Louise, Lotte and Frieda, and this time I was put in charge of the lighting. I burned myself slightly on Louise's flame – perhaps that was her revenge for what I'd said before – but I was com-pensated by the sight that appeared before me: the three siblings standing there, their faces lit from below, each holding their own mother lantern in front of their bellies, swelling and getting bigger and bigger, and then they let go, all three at the same time. Louise, Lotte and Frieda floated charmingly and elegantly after Joschi who, as a tiny dot of light, was by now hardly distinguishable from the other stars.

'Isn't that beautiful,' said Hannah.

'And now the children and Margit,' said my mother.

'Try and relax a bit,' said Hannah, waving after the mothers.

We were now a practised team. Gabor took Tamás, my mother Véra, I got Margit and Hannah the lighter. My mother carefully smoothed the paper of the lantern and said she owed her little big sister a perfect, wrinkle-free ascent, not least because of all the awful thoughts she had once had about Véra's red velvet dress. Gabor admitted he had no idea what Véra and Tamás had really looked like, and Hannah promised to make him copies of all the photographs still in existence.

When we released them into the sky, Margit's light strove resolutely upwards. Véra and Tamás's at first stayed nearby, but when Tamás's lantern suddenly veered off and described a wide curve to the left, Véra also freed herself from the lee of the mother ship and followed her brother's course. Together they looked like a dancing pair of eyes, heading eastwards.

'Take care, you two,' said my mother, and I looked for her hand and pressed it. 'And thanks again for everything. We haven't forgotten that we wouldn't even exist if you hadn't been killed.'

'I've never seen it that way,' Gabor said with amazement.

'Try it, it'll give you a whole new perspective on life,' said Hannah, but it didn't sound malicious, not even ironic.

'I'll think about it,' said Gabor, and bent down for the last three lanterns. 'Here's the one for Joschi's first—'

'Psst,' said my mother and clutched my hand more tightly. 'Did you hear that?'

No one moved. I held my breath, but I couldn't hear anything.

'What was it?' Hannah whispered.

'I thought I heard a voice,' my mother whispered back.

We waited for another while, but because nothing else happened, we agreed to set off the last three lanterns and then beat a swift retreat. We decided not to bother with the solemn deposition of Edgar's bouquet by the memorial of the Small Camp. It was fine where it was, in the grass, thought my mother. Hannah didn't see things quite like that, but she didn't want to put our special outing at greater risk.

In this last round, my mother took the lantern for Karl, Hannah the one for Mátild, Joschi's first wife, and I held Alfred in my hands. I tried to put myself in his shoes a bit, but it didn't work, and I felt as if Alfred didn't want to have anything to do with our ritual. Perhaps he'd rather have had a decent whisky. I was about to suggest that to my mother, but she was concentrating on Karl's lantern with such a loving expression on her face that I decided to leave it. After Gabor had lit all three fuel elements, I discovered a little tear in one of the side seams. I didn't pay much attention to it, particularly since Alfred's paper shell was starting to inflate at the same rate as the other two.

'I'm about to let go of mine,' Hannah announced.

'Wait,' I said. 'I'm not quite there.'

There was something up with Alfred. Or with me. I was just wondering whether it had to do with my ambivalent attitude towards him, when my mother suddenly said 'Up we go, Karl,' and let go. Hannah and I did the same.

Right then I knew that it had been a mistake. While Karl sped upwards, straight as an arrow, and Mátild followed in his wake without a moment's hesitation, Alfred's lantern started spinning after the first two or three metres of altitude, drifted to the right in the direction of the camp and then suddenly tilted to one side. At first it looked as if the flame had gone out, but then it flickered back to life and seemed to give the lantern another good upward shove. And then we saw it.

'Alfred's on fire,' my mother said.

'Oh shit,' said Hannah. 'Do you think he might do some sort of mischief here?'

I imagined Alfred setting the gate building on fire, a symbolic act of liberation and atonement. Perhaps I'd been underestimating him all this time.

'Everything's too damp,' said my mother. 'Come on, let's get out of here.'

'I think he's going to come down in a minute,' I said.

None of us managed to take our eyes off the burning Alfred in the dark night sky. He didn't just burn up, as I remembered our home-made lanterns in kindergarten doing, but seemed to have a system that kept him flying in spite of the flames for an astonishingly long time.

'He looks like the burning Hindenburg in Lakehurst,' Hannah remarked.

'What's that?' I asked.

'The temporary end of passenger airship travel,' said my mother. 'A Zeppelin that came to a nasty end in the thirties.'

'Watch out, now,' warned Gabor, who hadn't had anything to say on the matter so far.

Alfred's descent was almost comet-like compared to his flying. He just tipped over and burned up on the way down. We saw him disappear behind the tops of the trees. And then it was perfectly still for a moment.

'All right, come on then,' said my mother. 'Is any of our stuff still lying around?'

'Ten lanterns, scattered all over the grounds,' said Hannah.

'We can transfer some money to the memorial to pay for the clearing up,' my mother decided, and turned resolutely to go.

I turned round once more as we left the place where our birthday ritual for Joschi had taken place. I thanked the gods and the good spirits for their support. May all creatures be happy, whether dead or alive: I was, anyway. I looked at the trees all around, I looked into the dark night sky, I looked towards the gate building. I was saying farewell.

And then it was daylight.

Behind the trees a number of bright lights came to life and lit up the parade ground like a football stadium. Even here in our little patch of forest it was bright enough to make us freeze like startled deer. The light was intimidating and majestic at the same time. I should really have been scared, but I was just overwhelmed, and I could actually feel my grandfather jumping into the air with excitement. A Chinese lantern, all well and good, but here, on his hundredth birthday, the whole of Buchenwald was being lit up, and without a doubt that was far more to his taste.

I heard my mother beside me saying, 'Happy birthday, Joschi,' and knew that she had had exactly the same thoughts as I had. Gabor made a noise that sounded like Joschi's Serbian curse from before, and Hannah didn't make a sound. None of us moved. We stood there and awaited the things that lay ahead.

Alfred had practically landed on the bonnet of the watchman's van, we found out later. Alfred had given us away. Not true, my mother said. They'd spotted us long ago anyway.

# 16

BACK WE WENT, down the Ettersberg, and this time my mother was actually sitting next to me on the back seat. Even though it was still pitch-black outside, I imagined I was very familiar with the route by now: over there, behind the spot where the trees thinned out a little, the road must bend to the left. A little bit further on from there was the turn off to the belltower, which I hadn't had a chance to see all weekend. And a few bends beyond that the obelisk would be waiting for us, just as loyal and true and just as ugly as before, at the end of the road.

I turned around and looked out of the back window. The VW bus was maintaining a steady distance behind us. I wondered whether Hannah would dare to flirt with one of the police officers, or whether she hadn't already been doing so. I imagined Gabor wriggling with sheer embarrassment in his seat, while Hannah told the policeman with the curly black hair back in the bus about her survival training in the Negev Desert, hoping to discover some biblical antecedents on his part.

'I was in a squad car like that years ago,' my mother said to me under her breath. 'It was even bigger than the one behind us, I think.'

'What were you doing in it?'

'I was arrested after a demo against neo-Nazis. But they let us go straight away.'

The cap of the police officer at the wheel was on at a slight angle. Neither he nor his colleague said a single word during the journey. A voice on the radio called for a patrol car to go to a private party. I couldn't work out whether there was an enormous fight, or whether a neighbour had just complained to the police about the music.

'At first I suspect they thought we were Nazis as well,' I whispered. As obvious as it now seemed, that idea wouldn't have occurred to me all by myself. It was only when I saw the tense faces of the night watchmen and the police officers in the harsh floodlights that I worked out that – of course, they must have thought we were right-wing extremist vandals who had forced their way into the grounds and were getting up to some sort of idiotic mischief. Luckily the four of us made such a grotesque impression that very soon no one believed that we had weapons or other accomplices waiting in the undergrowth. From that point onwards, everything was very serious, matter of fact and workmanlike. One of the watchmen handed the policemen the charred Alfred like a trophy, and to my surprise Edgar's bouquet suddenly turned up as well, probably to be used as evidence. We would now be taken to Weimar police station, they said. I looked at the glaring lights of Buchenwald and wondered whether we were going to have to pay the electricity bill. I felt a bit intimidated, but I still wasn't scared. Perhaps that was because I was convinced I had ended up in the middle of the most exciting story of my life. I had even started to tell it to myself in my mind, while it was still happening, and experimenting with different ways of putting things.

We reached the edges of the city. I wondered whether I might one day incorporate blue lights, sirens and handcuffs into this story, and decided against it for the time being. My mother had a small, proud gleam on her face that was clearly something to do with the manner of her exit from Buchenwald. She held my hand, not because she wanted to console or reassure me, but because we were all so compatible that night.

My watch said ten past four. Our little convoy turned left into a driveway. On the sign outside the big, multi-storey building I could just read the words 'Weimar

Police Station' before we plunged into the underground car park. The policeman who had been driving the patrol car held the door open for me. Although he didn't make a big deal about it, I still thought his gesture was very kind. As we got out, Gabor gave me an encouraging smile and helped Hannah out of the VW bus. From this I concluded that Hannah had behaved properly on the way back.

The policemen escorted us along a staircase and several corridors until we arrived at an empty office that looked like any other office and nothing like the rooms you see on television, with recently arrested dealers and prostitutes. It smelled freshly renovated. The neon light made all the faces look very tired.

The recording of our personal details began. Thanks to my training in early evening TV series, I knew that we didn't have to give anything but the most basic information. The police on television kept trying it anyway, but to my amazement no one here asked us what was going on up on the Ettersberg and why, so I didn't even get to demand a lawyer I didn't have. I didn't even get to tell them my own date of birth and place of residence because my mother did it for me. It's pretty frustrating getting arrested with your mother, uncle and aunt when you're a minor – you're largely ignored.

Even Hannah was unusually taciturn and forgot to ask about the bouquet, as I had firmly expected her to do. Only Gabor, the last in line, seemed to feel the need to talk about the matter.

'You know, our father was a Jewish prisoner in Buchenwald,' he began. 'We wanted to celebrate his hundredth birthday there . . .'

Hannah and my mother wore identical facial expressions. For the first time I noticed that Hannah had mastered the trick with the raised eyebrows.

'You can give details of what happened when you are summoned to the relevant police station in your town of residence,' said the policeman, looking even more tired than before.

'Can you tell us what happens next? What we have to expect?'

'It all goes to the State Attorney's Office,' replied the policeman. We listened attentively.

'On charges of trespass?' My mother's locutions were always very precise, even just before dawn.

'No,' said the policeman, 'For desecration of graves. It's not a trivial matter.' His voice became a whole octave deeper and more significant as he said that and, strangely, he looked me straight in the eye for the first time as he did so. Perhaps he had guessed that I was the one responsible for spiritual affairs in the family.

On the way out we met the young policeman with the dark curls, who came towards us carrying a tray with three mugs of coffee. I saw the expression on Hannah's face. It had nothing to do with the coffee. So yes, I'd probably have been more interested if I hadn't been so worried about that desecration-of-graves stuff.

It was only when we were in the street that we realized our own car was still parked up in Buchenwald, and we had no idea where we were and how to get to our hotel from here. None of us really believed in the possibility of catching a cab in this city at five o'clock on a Sunday morning, so Hannah went back into the building and came back out a few minutes later with a very precise set of directions.

'Come on, kids, apparently it's only a ten-minute walk,' she said. 'I think that if it hadn't been against regulations, that young policeman would have been more than happy to walk me home.'

'You're nearly your old self again,' my mother observed.

'Desecration of graves, I can hardly believe it,' said Gabor, lighting a cigarette as he walked. 'Disturbing the peace of the dead. Of all the crimes I could ever have imagined committing, that would have been pretty well the last.'

'None of us desecrated anything,' said my mother stoutly when she saw my face. She stopped in front of me and rested her hands on my shoulders. 'Lily, perhaps we ignored the house rules, but we did respect the dead. I could even imagine the memorial management allowing our action.'

'If we'd asked first,' added Hannah.

'No, don't worry, Lily,' Gabor joined in. 'It was a really wonderful idea of yours. At worst we'll be fined, and it'll have been worth it.'

They were touchingly concerned about me, the three of them. When I thought about it, Buddhism didn't include the peace of the dead anyway: either you went on into the next round of existence or off into Nirvana, and in a state of enlightenment no one was going to be bothered by Chinese lanterns. We walked side by side in silence for a while. Hannah put her arm around me.

'But that business with the 10,000-watt lamps was just terrific,' Gabor said appreciatively.

'Terrific?' Hannah repeated. 'I nearly had a heart attack.'

'All boys like things like that, Hannah,' said my mother. 'If you tell Edgar about it, you must on no account leave that bit out.'

'Joschi would have liked it too,' I said.

Hannah laughed. 'I'd love to know what he'd have made of this story.'

'That's easy,' said my mother. 'It would have started with the lanterns being about three-metres long and staying in the air for a week.'

'A week?' said Gabor. 'That would have carried Alfred all the way to the marina at Rostock, where he'd have sunk someone's yacht.'

'We would have been arrested in handcuffs and carried off with blue lights and sirens,' I said, pretending the idea had just occurred to me.

'We'd have spent the whole night together in a cell,' Hannah cried enthusiastically. 'We'd have sung old

Zionist songs! And the next morning Gabor could have danced the Hora.'

'Hannah,' said my mother. 'Joschi would never have dreamed up a story in which I ended up hanging myself in a cell.'

We were getting on better and better, I thought. I looked around. The street we were walking along now struck me as vaguely familiar. The nose-flute shop and the playground with the Goethe Chestnut must have been around here somewhere as well. A man came towards us on a bicycle with a trailer full of Sunday papers.

'Jewish prisoner,' my mother said suddenly. 'You described Joschi as a Jewish prisoner, Gabor. Were you just trying to butter up the cops, or have you changed your mind after all?'

'It was pure coincidence that he said that,' Hannah said generously.

'Let's just leave it there, girls,' said Gabor. 'At this time of the morning people often say the strangest things.'

It was exactly half past five when we got to our hotel. Our farewell in the lobby was, in spite of the early hour, the longest so far. This was mostly because no one knew exactly whether and how he could hug one of the others without embarrassing one of the onlookers. Even Hannah, who my mother says used to hug trees, looked unusually shy.

It didn't matter. We promised each other that we

would appear on time for our last breakfast together, and I think we all felt pretty good when we parted.

Before I fell into bed, I turned my phone back on and set the alarm for ten o'clock. The display showed two missed calls and a text message from my father. I was too tired to read it, but I was glad.

'Dad sent me a text,' I said.

'Sleep well, Lily,' my mother said, and disappeared into the bathroom – where else.

# 17

FOUR HOURS LATER the sonar of my telephone located me in the middle of a confused dream about airships. I was alone. On the untouched half of the bed next to me lay a note with a request to pack my things together and come down for breakfast by eleven at the latest. I vaguely remembered that we had planned to travel home by train sometime around midday. My eye fell on Gabor's bear, which had slipped into the gap between the bed and the bedside table, and looked, with some justification, lonely.

'Hello, Bear,' I said. I pulled him out and smoothed his fur. He looked a bit benign for a Hungarian shepherd-bear, but Paul would love the story when he was old enough for it. I decided that the bear would be Paul's from now on.

Before I showered I read the message from my father inviting me for dinner this evening ('and ask your mother if she wants to come too'). I texted back to say that I would love to come and I would also ask my mother if she wanted to come as well, although I already knew her answer. At some point in the previous night I'd stopped dreaming about the two of them getting back together. I'd even stopped seeing that as the only possible happy ending.

In the bathroom I tried to increase my four hours of sleep to an imagined eight. To aid myself in this project, I used cold water, which I hardly ever do. To my amazement it actually helped. Afterwards I sat down for a while with my stone mandala, which was still spread out on the floor. Then I destroyed it. I brought the clay balls back to their flowerpot and put Joschi's stone in my pocket. The bear ended up at the top of my rucksack, from where he was able to look out. When I opened the door of the room to go downstairs, my mother was standing in front of me.

'I was about to come and get you,' she said.

We walked arm in arm to the lift. I looked down at our feet and noticed that we had the same walk. I looked up and discovered that I could look her straight in the eyes. That was new, or at least it had never struck me before.

'I've been up in Buchenwald with Hannah, fetching the car,' said my mother. 'Just imagine, someone had wedged a lily behind the windscreen wiper.'

I did imagine it. It wasn't difficult. It looked beautiful and forgiving. Then I tried to imagine what would have happened to me if my mother hadn't started every other sentence she said to me with the words 'Just imagine'.

'And, by the way, Hannah wants to take Gabor along in the car afterwards,' said my mother when the lift door had closed behind us.

Wow, I thought. 'Isn't that miles out of the way for her?'

My mother laughed. 'It is, but she claims that way at least she'll be able to sleep as long as he's driving. I don't believe a word of it.'

I liked the idea that none of us would be travelling back on our own.

Hannah and Gabor were already having breakfast. I thought Gabor didn't look like a maths teacher this morning, more like a weary anarchist. His ponytail wasn't as tight as usual, his skin looked a shade paler, if that was possible, but even though they were baggy his eyes flashed behind his aviator glasses when he saw us coming. Hannah looked equally weary, but very contented. Her bright red lipstick helped. For simplicity's sake, and because I felt like it anyway, I immediately hugged them both by way of greeting.

'Hello, Lily,' said Gabor. 'Get some sleep?'

'Yes, thanks,' I said, and sat down next to him. Gabor had divided his breakfast plate into four precise quadrants, and placed a food sample from the buffet on each of them. It looked like the set-up for an experiment. I remembered the bear, which had since this morning been a Hungarian shepherd bear. I pointed to my rucksack. 'Would you mind if I passed him on to my little brother?'

'What little—' Gabor began, broke off and then merely looked at my mother. It wasn't the ideal start for a relaxed morning-after breakfast. I had assumed that Gabor knew about Paul, although a moment later it was clear to me that that was complete nonsense. As if it hadn't been demonstrated emphatically enough to me that weekend, information doesn't spread by osmosis in a family.

Luckily Hannah is usually inspired by situations that most people would find embarrassing. 'Hey, we could draw up a checklist,' she suggested, and waved her serviette around. 'Everyone writes down on a sheet of paper what the other members of the family still really want to know about them. The list is updated once a year. And then if one of us dies, the others won't have to do so much guessing.'

'How sensible,' said my mother. 'And after you die we'll just give your list to the rabbi for his address, if you've managed to get a place in the Jewish cemetery by then.' She turned to Gabor. 'Lily's father had another child this year, you know.' She said it for the first time without that exaggerated cheerfulness that I'd always hated so much. She said it quite simply. End of.

'Of course the list would be only for private use,'

Hannah protested. 'You should invite my lovers rather than making the rabbi list them all. And besides, Gabor and I are going to outlive you anyway.'

'I like the idea,' said Gabor. 'Particularly since I don't have a Lily to tell all my stories to.'

'My mother uses me as an external hard drive for her memories,' I said, trying to look like a victim.

'Exactly,' confirmed my mother and poured us some coffee. 'You're my data back up.'

I went to the breakfast buffet three times in all, and I was so starving that I didn't even spurn the scrambled eggs in the warming pan that Gabor had gauged to be a health risk. We were the last guests in the dining room. A lady from the hotel staff had started clearing the cutlery from the nearby tables, and was noisily straightening the chairs. Then we saw her coming over with a vacuum cleaner and looking around for a socket.

'Oh God Almighty, we're about to go,' muttered Hannah.

Gabor straightened his ponytail and got up from his chair. Then he went over to the woman. 'I'm sorry,' he said. 'We've had a family reunion in your hotel this weekend and we'd like to say goodbye in peace. Would you please give us another ten minutes?'

My mother and Hannah exchanged appreciative glances.

'Of course,' said the woman and let go of the plug. The cable clattered swiftly back into the vacuum cleaner and concluded its journey with a loud clack as the plug struck the plastic.

'And now ask her for her phone number, go on, do it,' whispered Hannah.

'Far too soon,' my mother whispered. 'Wait till she comes back.'

Gabor gave the woman a weary-anarchist smile and came back to our table. 'What's up?' he asked when he saw our faces.

'Doesn't matter,' said Hannah.

'I don't want to know either,' said Gabor and sat down again. I couldn't help thinking of Peggy from the pizzeria and her budgie, and the fact that that evening was less than two days ago.

'So if Marika continues to refuse, I will deliver a short address,' Hannah said suddenly. 'I always feel so solemn when a parting is imminent.'

Gabor automatically reached for the cigarettes in his jacket pocket, then shrugged regretfully and leaned back with a calm expression.

'I'll keep it short, Gabor,' said Hannah. She bent down and took from her handbag a lily that had clearly spent the night under a windscreen wiper. 'But we need a bit of atmosphere.' She put the flower in Gabor's water glass, where it immediately toppled over.

'Never mind. So, my dears, and above all dear Joschi,' Hannah began. 'First of all I must admit that I came here with rather high expectations. I had hoped I'd finally be able to close up a few gaps in my knowledge. That I might resolve my relationship with my father and also have enough time to remain in phone contact with Edgar. Somehow none of that worked. Instead I've got the State Attorney's office on my back.'

I saw the vacuum-cleaner lady leaning casually against the wall behind the breakfast buffet. She was listening closely to Hannah's words. The swing door to the kitchen beside her opened, and Sammy poked his head into the room. The vacuum-cleaner lady whispered something to him. Sammy disappeared again.

'But instead I've got rid of something,' said Hannah, and suddenly her face looked different, much softer and more vulnerable than usual. 'All the ghosts that I've been carrying around with me all my life long. I saw them flying away last night, one after the other. There were more than ten, believe me. There were hundreds, perhaps even a few million. They weren't just the ghosts from my private family album, but also the ghosts from my books of photographs and the ghosts from my head. I have said farewell to them and let them go. And it was so easy! Lily, I'd have myself arrested any time for your Chinese-lantern idea, I really would.'

I realized that I was about to burst into tears.

'And now, one more thing for you, Joschi. I know you left our mothers with more than just a pile of bleak memories. And you also left your children with more than a few blurred trails and open questions. We're just discovering that now. Thank you for your stories. Thank you for this family. *Yom Huledet Same'ach* – Happy birthday, Joschi.'

For a moment it was perfectly quiet. Then Gabor, my mother and I started clapping like mad, while Sammy managed to get through the swing door with a lot of bluster and a tray. On the tray were a bottle of Sekt and four glasses. Clearly the vacuum-cleaner lady had quietly organized the whole thing, and luckily she'd been in charge of Sammy's timing as well. My mother and Hannah hugged each other, then Gabor threw himself in between them, and I stood a bit outside the whole thing, but that was fine too. Hannah's mobile coughed away unattended, and I had the surprise of the day when Sammy handed me a glass of Sekt, full to the brim, and on the house of course, as he assured us. When Hannah, Gabor and my mother parted at last, glasses were finally raised to Joschi in broad daylight. And our last farewell couldn't have been more hectic, once my mother realized that our train left in fifteen minutes.

# *18*

ON THE WAY BACK IN the train I remembered an old Joschi story.

When it happened, my mother must have been about seven years old. She came home from school at midday with a sore stomach. It was a real sore stomach, not the kind you sometimes get spontaneously when there's something unpleasant on the table, like stew. Unfortunately everything came together at once that day: a real sore stomach, stew and to top it all off an unusually ruthless Joschi, who thought he had spotted a fake stomach upset. Floating around in the stew amidst globules of fat were lots of alphabet noodles: a wretched attempt to improve matters, and one that didn't work: halfway through my mother threw up everything she had eaten so far under Joschi's severe gaze, all over the kitchen floor.

Joschi reacted with great consternation, and put my mother to bed before going back into the kitchen to clear everything up. Then he went back to my mother's bedroom and apologized for the fact that clearing up had taken so long, but after all she'd puked up a whole story on the kitchen floor, a very exciting story, and one with a number of instalments. Unfortunately he had had to clear it away, but obviously he had remembered the story, in case my mother wanted to hear the first instalment.

The contents of the vomited story has not been handed down. My mother said she almost fell out of bed laughing, but she could remember nothing more than that.

A few days later, at her insistence, they repeated the scene with a fresh pack of alphabet noodles on the kitchen table. My mother said that even at the age of seven she didn't, of course, hold out much hope that a story would come out of it, but there was just that tiny possibility, wasn't there? She stood next to Joschi at the table, staring through screwed-up eyes at the sea of alphabet noodles and couldn't even spot a simple word like 'car' or 'flower' or 'hat'. She told Joschi. He looked at her in surprise for a moment, then turned towards the mountain of noodles and started reading out loud. It was the story of an eraser that had fallen in love with a bicycle tyre – my mother remembers the story very clearly, because she was desperately trying all the while to find the words that Joschi was, in spite of his broken German, effortlessly and fluently lining up beside one another. A jealous dynamo came into the story as well. 'And then dynamo peel tyre like apple,' Joschi read, and at that point my mother gave up once and for all, because she didn't know how to spell 'dynamo'. It only occurred to her much later that Joschi probably had no more of an idea than she had.

At that moment I realized that I had found a way into my presentation. I saw the pile of alphabet noodles, I saw the glass case from Buchenwald with all the buttons in it, and all of a sudden I knew that where chaos has been left behind, stories are waiting. You just had to put things in the right order.

I wanted to ask my mother why she hadn't told that story during our weekend, when it would have fitted so brilliantly, but my mother's head was half-buried in her coat and she seemed to be asleep. I watched her carefully for a while and came to the conclusion that she actually was sleeping. That upset me slightly. I was about to send my father a message ('Mum's asleep on public transport'), because I thought for a moment that if she could do something like that she might love him again. But in the end I left things as they were, and wondered instead whether I should give bathtubs and space capsules another chance in my life. And besides, I suddenly had an overwhelming desire to learn Hebrew.

# Acknowledgements

I WOULD LIKE TO THANK Daniel Gaede and the staff of Buchenwald Memorial for their kind support with my research – and for one particularly enlightening clue.